Lily Quench

and the Black Mountains

Lily Quench

and the Black Mountains

NATALIE JANE PRIOR

Illustrations by Janine Dawson

PUFFIN BOOKS

Happy 70th Birthday, Dad (Gordon)
October 6, 2001

PUFFIN BOOKS
Published by Penguin Group
Penguin Young Readers Group,
345 Hudson Street, New York, New York 10014, U.S.A.
Penguin Books Ltd, 80 Strand, London WC2R ORL, England
Penguin Books Australia Ltd, 250 Camberwell Road, Camberwell, Victoria 3124, Australia
Penguin Books Canada Ltd, 10 Alcorn Avenue, Toronto, Ontario, Canada M4V 3B2
Penguin Books (N.Z.) Ltd, 182-190 Wairau Road, Auckland 10, New Zealand

First published in Australia and New Zealand by Hodder Headline Australia Pty Limited,
a member of the Hodder Headline Group, 2001
Published by Puffin Books, a division of Penguin Young Readers Group, 2004

1 3 5 7 9 10 8 6 4 2

LIBRARY OF CONGRESS CATALOGING-IN-PUBLICATION DATA

Prior, Natalie Jane, 1963-
Lily Quench and the Black Mountains / Natalie Jane Prior ; illustrations by Janine Dawson.
p. cm.
Summary: Lily Quench and her friend Queen Dragon trek to the treacherous Black
Mountains to find the rare blue lily, the necessary ingredient for a potion to help protect the
kingdom of Ashby from the Black Count and his armies.
ISBN 0-14-240021-1
[1. Dragons—Fiction. 2. Fantasy.] I. Dawson, Janine, ill. II. Title.
PZ7.P9373Li2004 [Fic]—dc22 2003058433

Printed in the United States of America

The Black Mountains

chapter one

The Return of the Count

It was snowing.

Across the knife's-edge peak of the Black Mountains a wind blew, eddying snowflakes down into the Valley of the Citadel. The wind whistled through the chinks in the walls of the miners' huts and shredded the plumes of smoke that struggled from the chimneys of the soldiers' barracks. In the courtyard of the Black Citadel a gang of workers in thin clothes battled to clear a heap of snow that had slid off the guardhouse roof. A few fires burned like teardrops at the guard posts, but that was all.

From his turret window, Gordon watched for his father to come home. Although he had given orders that he was to be told as soon as the armored car cleared the pass, he could not help longing for the first glint of headlights on the road. His bedroom was dark, except for the fire burning on the hearth and a lamp by his bed, but outside no stars were visible because of the blizzard. In the Black Mountains, winter lasted longer than anywhere else, so that there never seemed to be anything but snow.

Gordon was warm. His floor was covered with a thick, richly patterned carpet, there was hot chocolate warming on a trivet, and he had just eaten a delicious dinner of soup, steak, chips, and ice cream. Despite this, he felt restless. His father should have been home hours before. Gordon wanted to tell him about the three bull's-eyes he had scored at target practice, about the latest news from the weapons factory, and about the strange way Angela had been behaving since he had left for the Ashby border. Impatiently, Gordon opened the window and stuck out his head. The cold hit him like a hammer, howling and whistling and striking at his cheeks with a thousand tiny, stinging blows.

Suddenly, Gordon yelled and ducked. A huge dark shadow had swooped down out of nowhere and passed directly overhead. Although it was gone as quickly as it had appeared, a wave of warm air passed swiftly over him and a spatter of water hit his upturned face. It was melted snowflakes, and, although they began to freeze again almost immediately, there was something else, too: a scent of something hot, oily, and metallic that lingered after the heat had passed and was too strong for him to have possibly imagined.

For a moment longer, Gordon hung out of the window, willing the strange apparition to come back. He was not frightened exactly, but he was curious and wanted to know what he had seen. He could only guess it was some sort of armored flying machine. But the vision was gone. No alarm sounded from the watchtowers, the sentry walked his beat below him, and then, on the mountain pass below, he saw the first flickering headlights and knew that his father was nearly home.

High on a crag above the Black Citadel, Lily Quench struggled down from her dragon's mouth and wrapped her fireproof cape tightly around her. Although she and Queen Dragon were the best of friends, there was still, she thought, something a bit unnerving about sitting on a dragon's scaly tongue. Ordinarily when they traveled she sat on Queen Dragon's head, but the storms in the Black Mountains were so wild she would have been ripped off in an instant. In the dragon's mouth it was at least warm, which was more than could be said for the spot where they now perched.

Lily huddled in the crook of Queen Dragon's foreleg and lifted her night goggles to her eyes. Even with them it was hard to see anything for the storm, but luckily Queen Dragon's eyesight was better than hers.

Suddenly the dragon dropped her head, hunkering down behind the crag. "Sssh!" she said.

Lily fell to her knees, crawled forward a few paces, and peered between some rocks.

Through her goggles, she saw a line of

headlights coming up the pass, the whine of straining engines cutting thinly through the wind. Two tanks came first, followed by some motorcycles, a sleek armored car with caterpillar treads on the wheels, and two more outriders bringing up the rear. The procession reached the top of the pass and drove right past them, slowly winding its way down into the valley on the other side.

"Creep," muttered Queen Dragon as the Black Count's armored car passed them. She had picked up the expression recently from an acquaintance back in Ashby Water, and become stuck on it. "Creep. One fireball, that's all he needs. He'd be fried alive."

"No, Queen Dragon," said Lily firmly. "You know what we were told. Our mission is just to find out what's happening. We can't do anything else until King Lionel tells us to."

"Humph," said Queen Dragon. "Well, you know what I think. Haven't we seen enough to act? Besides, this place gives me the willies." She looked unhappily at the rocks of Dragon's Neck, towering behind them. "Just being here makes my scales stand on end."

"Me, too," said Lily. She shivered, not merely from the cold. "Let's go. If we leave now, we can be back in Ashby Water by morning."

A few moments later, the crag above the pass was empty again. Far above it, a tiny dark shape circled once and flew away to the east. Down in the valley, the armored car and its escort reached the citadel. The great iron gate opened slowly, like an enormous mouth, and it drove inside.

In his audience chamber in the citadel, the Black Count stripped off his leather gloves and laid them on the table. He took a key out of his pocket and unlocked the huge iron box his servants had set before him. Inside was what looked to be a scorched and buckled car tire, a sheaf of photographs bound between two crimson boards, and a woman's black leather shoe.

The count sat down on a tall carved chair. He was not a big man, nor particularly handsome or distinguished looking. But somehow, when he opened his mouth, people took the trouble to hear what he was saying in his soft voice, and when he walked into a room its occupants fell back and were silent. The count held a dozen countries in his power; had conquered nations, towns, and kingdoms; and sent whole cities up in flames. Hardly anyone in his empire did not tremble when they thought of him, or quake at the mention of his name.

The door opened. "You sent for me, Your Eminence?"

"Come in, Sark," said the count, and General Sark, commander of the Black Squads, clicked his heels and entered the room. When he reached the table and saw the open box, he stopped and looked surprised.

"That's all that's left of the car, Your Eminence?"

"I'm afraid so," said the count. "We believe Zouche's assistant was trying to return to the citadel to warn us when she was attacked. By something very powerful, very dangerous."

He handed Sark the photographs. The general looked through them quickly. His face grew paler with every picture.

"It's incredible. I've never seen anything like it."

"Nor have I," said the count. "As you can see,

this makes the Ashby situation far more serious than we realized. Have you had any more reports while I've been gone?"

"None," said General Sark. "I'm afraid our spies in Ashby have deserted us."

"There will still be someone," said the count. "There always is. Track them down, Sark. Learn what is happening in Ashby and find out exactly what their secret weapon is. We must obtain one ourselves—several if possible. Then we will launch an immediate attack on Ashby Water and crush this revolt as it deserves." He looked up, disturbed by a scratching at the door. "Come in, Gordon. I didn't realize you were still up."

The door opened a second time, and Gordon came in. "I was waiting for you," he said, and for a split second it was on the tip of his tongue to tell his father about the thing he had seen flying over the citadel. But then he saw the expression on General Sark's face and stopped.

The count reached out his hand for Gordon's. Even though he had been out in the snow, his fingers were warm to the touch. "What were you going to say, my son?"

Gordon yanked his attention back. "N–nothing,

Father," he stammered. "Only—I got three bull's-eyes at target practice this morning. I thought you'd like to know."

"Your Excellency can't be finding the Boys' Squad much of a challenge nowadays," said General Sark slyly, and Gordon hated him for it. "Three bull's-eyes! At this rate you will be commanding your own Black Squad before the year is out."

"That's for my father to decide," said Gordon rudely. Something about General Sark always made him uncomfortable, and he wished with all his heart he would go away. But he could see from the preoccupied expression on his father's face that tonight this wasn't going to happen.

"Time enough for the real army later," said the count. "I would not like to push Gordon into something he is not ready for, particularly when I might be occupied somewhere else." His eyes returned to the table, and for the first time Gordon saw the photographs of the twisted wreckage on the Ashby road: the pathetic remains of a sports car that, if he had only known it, had been mostly eaten by the same dragon he had just seen flying over the citadel.

"There's going to be a war, isn't there?" he said, and did not know whether to be excited or not.

The Black Count smiled at him. "My son," he said, "somewhere, there always is."

chapter two

King Lionel's Council

"Rats!" said Lily Quench in a disappointed voice. "That's the last of it."

She looked at Jason, and Jason Pearl looked at her. On the oak table between them a glass flask fizzed over a Bunsen burner. Green smoke rose up from it, and there was black sticky gunk on Lily's bedroom ceiling. It would all have looked very spectacular—only fizz, green smoke, and gunk wasn't what they'd been trying to get.

"You've wrecked my chemistry set," said Jason crossly.

"Bother your chemistry set. You were the one

who wanted to do it," retorted Lily. "I told you there weren't enough petals. Besides, you can always get another chemistry set, but finding another blue lily for making Quenching Drops is a different matter altogether." She shook out her handkerchief, and a few flakes of faded blue petal floated like goldfish food onto the floor. A faint scent still clung to them, but there was no pretending there were enough for another try.

"You must be able to get the petals somewhere," said Jason. "After all, your grandmother had them in her Quenching Trunk. She must have discovered them on her travels."

"I guess so," said Lily. "My mother was a gardener, and I thought she might have grown them. But when I went to the Botanic Gardens, the new head gardener had never seen anything like them in Ashby."

"Could Queen Dragon help?" suggested Jason.

"She's more likely to get offended," said Lily. "Quenching Drops were invented to kill dragons, remember? If I told her we were trying to make some, she'd probably be very upset."

Lily put her grandmother's recipe book back into her wardrobe, along with her sword and fireproof cape. She thought back to the days when she and her grandmother had lived together here in the house beside the grommet factory. If there was a nook or cranny she had not searched in, Lily couldn't remember it. Old Ursula's patchwork cat smiled at her from her bed, as if it knew something she didn't. Then, from Ashby Castle across the way, a single bell started to sound.

"Come on, Jason," said Lily. "We'd better go. King Lionel's Council is about to meet."

King Lionel of Ashby had not been king for long. In fact, he had often wondered whether he would ever become king at all. For ten years while the Black Count's armies ruled his kingdom, Lionel had been in hiding. First, as a little boy he had been smuggled out of Ashby by Lily's grandmother, Ursula Quench. Then he had returned in secret as a grown-up and worked in the castle library, planning for the day his kingdom would be free.

It had been a hard job, dangerous and

frightening. At any time, Lionel's true identity could have been exposed, his plans uncovered, his precious books and manuscripts thrown into the grommet factory blast furnace. Every night when he went to bed, he had heaved a sigh of relief that he had made it through another day. Yet now he was finally king, things didn't seem much better. Lionel's subjects were poor, his kingdom was in ruins, and the Black Count's army was likely to return at any moment. Sometimes, only the thought of his wife, Queen Evangeline, gave Lionel the strength to carry on.

What he didn't know was that Evangeline was even more scared than he was.

Queen Evangeline was with him now in the throne room, dressed in a plain red dress and with a worried crease across her forehead. Around the table sat the other Royal Councillors: Jason Pearl; Mr. Hartley, the minister of the Ashby Church; and Lily Quench, who had crowned him only a few months before. The last member of the council, Queen Dragon, was too big for the room, so she sat in the castle courtyard looking in through the window. In the cool spring weather her warm dragonish breath was as good as central heating.

Lionel looked at the portrait of his father, King Alwyn, which had recently replaced the one of the Black Count on the throne room wall. He drew a deep breath and began.

"Ladies and gentlemen," he said, "as everyone knows, it is now six months since the Black Count's armies were defeated. Ever since, Queen Evangeline and I have worried the count might return. Last week, we decided to ask our official Quencher, Duchess Lily, to make a secret trip to the Black Mountains to find out what the count is planning. Duchess Lily, would you like to report on your mission?"

"Your Majesty." Lily stood up and bowed politely. "Fellow councillors, I'm afraid that what Queen Dragon and I discovered is rather worrying. First of all, more than a hundred Black Squads have been marched down from the mountains to the Ashby border. And second, the Black Count himself has been making inquiries about what is happening here.

"After the Battle of Ashby Church, when our enemy Miss Moldavia was killed trying to escape, most of the Black Squads in Ashby decided to stay here. All except one squad, which was searching for Queen Dragon in Ashby Thicket. When Queen Dragon gave them the slip, they escaped home to the Black Empire."

"They've given the count what was left of Miss Moldavia's sports car," interrupted Queen Dragon. "The one I mostly ate. It seems I missed a few little bits. I was in a hurry," she added apologetically.

"Don't worry, Queen Dragon," said Lily. "It wasn't your fault. Anyway, the count has taken the car parts back to the Black Citadel. It seems he thinks Queen Dragon is some sort of secret weapon belonging to King Lionel, and he's decided he has to do something about it. Unless we act quickly, by Christmas Ashby Water will be invaded and we will all be the Black Count's prisoners."

"I'd rather be dead," said Queen Evangeline.

"We probably will be," said King Lionel gloomily. "Ashby has no weapons, no army. Only a few former Black Squadders, and some grommeteers who don't know how to fight."

"I'm sure it's not that bad, Your Majesty," said Jason in an encouraging voice. "If we put our minds to it, we might be able to strike at the count before he strikes us."

"Queen Evangeline and I will discuss the matter further," said King Lionel. "Meanwhile, we have another item of business to attend to. Sir Jason, would you please show in Mrs. Crystal Bright?"

"I'll show myself in, thank you," said a voice. The throne room door banged open, and a plump woman with sharp-looking teeth and purple-streaked hair swept into the room. She marched up to the queen. "Evangeline, do you realize how long you've kept me waiting? A fine thing, miss, to leave your mother standing in the corridor like some grommeteer waiting for a bus."

Evangeline looked uncomfortable. Lionel stood up and politely pulled out a chair. Evangeline's mother immediately sat down on his throne.

"That's better," she said. "A bit of respect, that's all I ask. Which leads me to the matter I've come here to discuss. As Queen Mother, I think it's high time we arranged my coronation."

"Your coronation!" exclaimed Evangeline. "Mother, what are you talking about? You can't be crowned! The Queen Mother is the mother of the king, not the queen."

Crystal swung her foot under her designer

gown. "Hoity-toity," she said. "What's the difference? I'm sick of all these excuses. Someone's got to take advantage of this miserable situation. Just look at you. Queen of Ashby! You should be wearing silk and ermine and dripping with jewels. You were better dressed when you were plain Miss Bright."

"I know she was, ma'am," said King Lionel quietly. "But you see, Ashby is very poor right now. It wouldn't be fair if the king and queen wore jewels when some of their subjects have hardly enough to eat."

"Pooh!" said Crystal. "Grommeteers! Why worry about them? We never did before." She stood up and turned to her daughter. "I'm giving you fair warning, Evangeline. I want a crown and a coronation, and if I don't get them you'll be sorry. As far as I'm concerned, that husband of yours is a joke. King Lionel! What a twerp! We Brights were better off by far under the Black Count."

She left the room, and, for a moment, the councillors sat in silence. Queen Evangeline's face was white, but her nose was turning red, and she reached for her handkerchief. King Lionel took her hand and squeezed it.

"Ladies and gentlemen," he said, "I think we'd better call this meeting to a close."

The Royal Library filled most of the South Turret of Ashby Castle. It was a large room with high vaulted ceilings painted blue and gold and whitewashed walls lined with neat shelves of books. Contented visitors sat reading in quiet corners, and the librarians and their assistants went cheerfully about their work, but this had only recently been the case. During the Black Count's first invasion, the library had been set on fire, and not so long ago, Miss Moldavia's Black Squads had ransacked and nearly destroyed it. Lily looked at the pile of ancient books on the table in front of her and sighed. Though King Lionel's dedication had restored them to the library, so far not a single page she had read had mentioned the blue lily.

A footstep sounded beside her. "Still searching?" asked Lionel.

Lily nodded. "It's as if the blue lily never existed," she said. "Only it must have, because we know it's what Quenching Drops are made from.

If we could just find where they grow, we could make as many drops as we wanted. Granny's recipe says they can be used against anything made of metal, as well as dragons, so we could use them on the Black Count's tanks."

"That would certainly come in handy," agreed Lionel. "As a matter of fact, Lily, I've just remembered something that might help with your search. Come with me, and I'll show you."

Lionel led Lily through a tiny door and up a winding staircase to a room in the very top of the turret. It was not much bigger than her own castle bedroom, and contained a desk, a chair, lots of bookcases, and a squashy blue sofa by the fireplace for cozy reading.

"This is my private sitting room," said Lionel, closing the door. "Evangeline and I come here when we want to be quiet—and when we want to consult the Ancient Chronicles of Ashby." As he spoke, he took a key from around his neck and unlocked a small cupboard in the turret wall. Inside Lily could just see half a dozen leather-bound books, a gold box, and a folded piece of parchment.

Lionel took out the box and sat beside Lily on

the sofa. He pressed an enameled flower on the lid, and a hidden catch clicked open. Inside was a square of faded blue silk, embroidered with the royal motto, "By Quenching We Rule." Underneath it was a small ancient book with a black cover and cracked spine.

"This is one of Ashby's greatest treasures," said Lionel solemnly. "It is the diary of your five times great-grandmother, Matilda Quench the Drakescourge, the same one who killed two dragons with a single catapult shot. What you might not know is where that famous fight took place."

"Where did it happen?"

"In the Black Mountains," said Lionel, "in the valley called Dragon's Downfall, beyond the Black Citadel. Matilda describes it all here. If you look"—he turned the brittle pages carefully—"you'll see it was there that Matilda first found the blue lily, which is the main ingredient in Quenching Drops."

He passed the book to Lily. Matilda's writing was thick and bold and sprawled all over the page. When she got excited, her pen tore right through the paper and splattered ink in great black blotches. As Lily read how Matilda had tracked down the dragons to their mountain lair, she felt the scaly patch on her elbow start to tingle. But then, just as Matilda crossed over the mountains and lured the dragons into Dragon's Downfall, the writing suddenly became an unreadable scrawl. Lily squinted at the page.

"I can't read this bit. What does she say?"

"I'm not sure, exactly," said Lionel. "There's something at the beginning about danger and a golden child. And this word here is definitely 'bones.' Matilda says she found the blue lily in a place where there were bones. Then we turn the page, and there's this funny doodle like a tooth with a hole through it. After that, the writing becomes easy to read again. See, here she is, writing about the great fight with the twin dragons."

But Lily was no longer interested in Matilda's fight. The days when the Quenches had been dragon slayers were long past; now they had other, even more dangerous enemies. She put down the book and stood up.

Far away, outside her beloved cottage on the Island of Skansey, the apple blossom would be out and the bulbs she had planted in the autumn would be starting to flower. The sheep would have had their lambs. But however much she wanted to fly back there and be part of it, as a Quench, Lily knew she had two homes. She belonged to Ashby, too. And as a Quench, she had to do whatever she must to stop the Black Count's return.

"Your Majesty," she said, "this is a job for your official Quencher, isn't it?"

Lionel nodded. "I think this is a situation which needs bravery and cunning, like the Quenches of old."

"Then Queen Dragon and I will go back to the Black Mountains," said Lily. "We will find the blue lily, and, if we can, we will stop the Black Count from invading. Ashby will be safe. As the last of the Quenches, Your Majesty, you have my word."

chapter three

Liza's Secret

Lily did not tell anybody about her new expedition. She and Lionel agreed it was better kept a secret for a little while, even from Queen Dragon and Evangeline. Over the next few weeks they continued their research in the Royal Library, looking up every old book they could find on the Black Mountains and copying out the pages of Matilda's diary as best they could. They found a map of the Black Empire from the days when Miss Moldavia and Captain Zouche had ruled Ashby for the count. Then Lily found an even older one, which showed how things had been before the Black Empire ever existed.

"It's amazing," she said, running her hands over the ancient parchment. "Look at all these little countries! I've never even heard of most of them."

"That's because the Black Empire has swallowed them up," said Lionel. "All of them once had their own kings, queens, and governments. The Black Counts have conquered every one."

"How terrible." Lily remembered the grommet factory that had poured its smoke over Ashby Water, and the Black Squads that had terrorized the citizens. She had never realized how many other places had lived through the same experience. A strong tingle pricked her elbow at the thought that she could help. For the first time she started to feel excited about her quest.

That night, when Lily went home to Ursula's cottage, she found she could not sleep. Instead, she opened her window so she could smell the flowers in the Botanic Gardens next door and pulled her grandmother's Quenching Trunk out from under the bed. The trunk contained all that was left of her family's magical Quenching

Equipment, including the small wooden box that had once held Ursula's precious supply of blue lily petals and Quenching Drops. Lily had lost the drops herself some months earlier when Captain Zouche and Miss Moldavia had forced her to fight Queen Dragon at the grommet factory. She had dropped them in sheer terror in the grommet factory stockpile, and though she had often kicked herself since, the mistake was made now and could not be mended.

Lily wrapped the blue-and-green patchwork quilt Ursula had made for her around her shoulders and started to sort through the papers at the bottom of the trunk. There were notes on weaponry and travel, photos of her parents' wedding and her grandmother with King Alwyn, and a packet of letters going back over several generations of Quenches. For the umpteenth time, Lily read through them. There were bills for armor, fan mail to Jeffrey Quench from starstruck princesses, and requests for dragon slaying from countries far and wide. There was even a love letter from her grandmother to her grandfather that made Lily blush. But there was no mention anywhere of the blue lily, and, at last,

Lily bundled the letters together and tossed them back into the trunk. One caught in the frayed lining and the fragile material tore across.

"Rats!" Lily pulled the letter out. It was only then that she noticed something else that had slipped down into the gap. The object was a small brown notebook, missing most of its back cover and spotted with water drops as if it had been left out in the rain. Lily carefully fished it out. She opened the front cover and there, in bold writing on the flyleaf, was its owner's name:

LIZA

All at once, the scales on Lily's elbow started tingling more furiously than they had ever done before. Without being told, she knew that the notebook had been the property of her mother, Liza Cornstalk Quench, who had once worked in the Ashby Botanic Gardens. Lily started to turn the notebook's pages. They were full of jottings about rose pruning and bulb planting, but ten pages in, a dirty, water-stained sheet of paper had been stuck into the book. Lily read it through several times. Then she excitedly shoved the notebook into the pocket of her nightdress and rummaged in the wardrobe for her flashlight.

A few minutes later Lily was running through the Botanic Gardens to the Ashby Dragon House. She arrived to find a puff of sulfurous smoke curling out of its entrance, like a baby volcano. Sparks of fire glowed in the cracks of the rubble walls, and there was a sound of dragonish snoring inside. Lily shone her light over the engraved nameplate, which read **Sinhault Fierdaze: Queen Dragon—Private, No Admittance**, and rapped loudly on the metal with her flashlight.

"Queen Dragon? It's Lily. Are you awake?"

The snoring interrupted itself, and there was a loud yawn that sent a hot cloud of smoke shooting out the entrance. Lily coughed and flapped her hand in front of her face. She was not, of course, silly enough to go inside uninvited, which was the surest way to get squashed flat.

"Queen Dragon? It's me, Lily."

This time, a sleepy voice called out for her to come in. Lily drew a deep breath and walked inside.

By dragon standards, the Ashby Dragon House was a comfortable one. It had a high beehive roof with a chimney and a sleeping platform made of the old concrete floor of the grommet factory furnace room. Around the rubble walls of its single room were neat piles of iron grommets, rescued from the factory and sorted according to size and flavor. Like all dragons, Queen Dragon lived on metal and was known to get peckish in the night.

"Hello, Lily." Queen Dragon sat up and rubbed her eyes. Their yellow orbs glowed eerily in the darkness. "How can I help you? It's awfully late for you to be out."

"I've just learned something important," said Lily, and all at once she stopped. In her excitement, she had forgotten that Queen Dragon knew nothing about the blue lily or the Quenching Drops and that, furthermore, she might not think searching for the lily was such a good idea. But it was too late to stop now. She reached into her pocket and pulled out her mother's notebook.

"Queen Dragon, have you ever heard of the blue lily?"

"Nn-nooo," said Queen Dragon. "I can't say I have."

"Well," said Lily, "it's a plant. A very rare one. It was first found by my ancestor, Matilda Quench the Drakescourge—you remember, the one you said had pimples? It only grows in the Black Mountains, in one particular place."

"Oh," said Queen Dragon ominously. "And what did old crater face use it for?"

Lily bit her lip. "I'm afraid . . . to make Quenching Drops."

For a moment, Queen Dragon said nothing. She turned, if possible, an even deeper red than normal. Then, in a strangled voice, she said, "I thought you were my friend."

"Queen Dragon, I am!" Lily rushed forward and clambered up Queen Dragon's scaly leg. It was impossible to put an arm around any portion of her giant body, so instead she went down on her knees and laid her cheek against her scales. "I am your friend! I would never use Quenching Drops against you! But the Black Count is going to invade Ashby again, and Lionel and I thought the drops might work against the Black Squads. See this notebook? It was written by my mother. She says she grew blue lilies from a bulb my grandmother brought back from the Valley of Dragon's Downfall—"

"No!" Queen Dragon started up like a scaly earthquake, and Lily pitched off her foreleg onto the concrete floor. "Not there! You're not making me go to that dreadful place!"

"But Queen Dragon, why ever not?" cried Lily. "It's just a Quenching Expedition. We've been through lots of worse adventures."

"Nothing's as bad as Dragon's Downfall," said Queen Dragon. "I won't do it; I won't!" As she spoke, she shifted agitatedly from one foot to the other, and her giant tail beat an anxious tattoo on the floor. Then, before Lily could say another word, she rushed out of the dragon house, flapped her wings, and flew away.

In the Black Mountains, far away, Gordon awoke in the cold early-morning darkness. The fire in his bedroom had burned low during the night, and a sprinkle of snow was falling outside. Gordon did not care. He jumped out of bed and reached excitedly for his clothes. The night before, his father had promised to spend the whole day with him.

It was going to be the best birthday he'd ever had.

In the sitting room, his breakfast had been laid out by the servants, together with his birthday presents. Most were from people who just wanted to suck up to the Black Count's son, but there was a hand-knitted red sweater from Angela, and a magnificent belt and dagger from his great-aunt Lucy, who was old and deaf and felt the cold too much to visit very often. Gordon buckled it on, and then the door opened and his father was there, dressed in his usual plain uniform with a greatcoat on, ready for going out.

"Have you finished your breakfast?" he asked, and Gordon nodded, though he had scarcely eaten a bite.

"Get your coat, then," said the count. "There's something I want to show you."

Gordon threw on his outdoor clothes. He and his father went together down the turret stairs, past the door that led out into the courtyard, and down to the cellars beneath the citadel. Then they went along a passage to a small garage Gordon had never even known existed. The count unlocked the door with a key and switched on the light.

In the middle of the garage stood a motorbike. It was not a scooter or a trail bike like the ones Gordon had ridden up until now, but a real racing bike painted gleaming black with a chromed engine and handlebars, backswept exhausts, and an instrumentation panel bristling with dials. It smelled of clean oil, rubber, and new leather. Last but not least, it had a sidecar shaped like a rocket.

"What do you think?" said the count. "Do you like it?"

"It's beautiful," breathed Gordon.

"It's yours," said the count simply, and he handed Gordon the key.

For a moment, Gordon was so stunned he did not know what to say. He could not believe that this wickedly beautiful piece of machinery was actually his. On one of the handlebars was a white envelope tied on with a red ribbon. He untied it mechanically and opened it: inside was a spare key and a simple note from his father wishing him a happy birthday. A lump came into his throat. He ran his fingers over the shiny metal handlebars.

"Thank you." Gordon could barely manage to get the words out, but the count simply smiled.

He unhooked the sidecar, took a pair of helmets off a shelf, and tossed one over.

"Shall we take it for a run?"

Gordon nodded. His father climbed onto the bike and kicked it into neutral. "I'll drive this time, if you don't mind," he said. "There's something I particularly want to show you. Besides, you haven't driven on the mountain roads before. It might be an idea to get some practice before you do."

He pulled on his helmet and Gordon hopped onto the seat and handed back the key. The count opened the garage door and started the ignition with a roar. Exhaust fumes filled the garage and the bike shot out of the opening like a wild animal. The sound of its engine split the frosty air. And at that moment it seemed to Gordon that there was no one in the world who was luckier or happier than he was.

chapter four

Gordon's Birthday

Gordon had no idea where his father was taking him. He simply enjoyed the ride while it lasted, looking at the scenery and relishing the chance of a holiday. The bike had a heated seat and his leather coat and gloves were lined with fur, but it was still incredibly cold, and the mountain winds buffeted him until every muscle in his body ached.

The bike roared out of the low wide tunnel that cut under the Dragon's Neck peak, and the count turned off onto a side road. After about ten minutes, they drove up to a squat gray building surrounded by a barbed-wire fence. At the sight of the factory, Gordon felt disappointed, but of course he didn't show it. They pulled up in the directors' parking lot, and a man in a gray coat came down the front step of the main building.

"Welcome, Your Eminence. The test is scheduled for half an hour." He showed them inside and offered them hot drinks out of a machine. While Gordon drank a cup of hot chocolate, the count asked a lot of questions about productions and schedules and whether something was going to be ready by the summer.

"Ah. You want a squadron for the Ashby campaign," said the man, who was the factory director.

The count shook his head. "No. I want three squadrons. Four would be better." He looked at his watch. "Come on, Gordon. We've just got time to have a look inside the factory."

"Your Eminence." The director bowed, but Gordon saw he did not look happy at all.

Together the three of them went through a door into an enormous factory. It was filled with metal gantries, overhead lifts, and machinery. An army of workers was clustered around a dozen gleaming black metallic shapes, busily riveting and welding.

"Are they tanks?" Gordon asked his father, but the count shook his head. He climbed some stairs onto an overhead walkway and leaned over the railing, watching the work progress with keen dark eyes.

Mystified, Gordon followed him. The director had given him earmuffs, but the noise was still deafening, and there were so many workers on the factory floor it was hard to see exactly what was being built. Some of the shapes were little more than metal skeletons; but one had what looked to be a head, and another had a strange pointed tail. In another part of the factory, a separate group of workers busied themselves with what looked to be several enormous bats' wings. Gordon turned to ask the director what they were, but as he opened his mouth, a siren blared, and somebody started talking incomprehensibly through a loudspeaker.

"Time for the test, Your Eminence," said the director, and he led the count and Gordon up another flight of stairs and through a door out onto the factory roof. They went over to the edge and stood, waiting and watching, behind a railing.

It was a minute or two before Gordon heard anything. Then there was a metallic rattle like the sound of a garage door going up and a low buzz that grew slowly more and more urgent. Gordon looked around to see where it was coming from. Suddenly there was a blast of foul-smelling exhaust, and a black object about the size of a small tank shot out of the building below, flapping wings and streaming fire in its wake.

"Wow!" Gordon was so excited he nearly fell over the railing. "It flies! It's fantastic! Father, can I have a go in one?"

"Maybe later when we've done some more test flights." The count looked amused. "Not today, at any rate. It's called a dragonet. Do you like it?"

"I think it's brilliant." While Gordon watched, the machine pulled in its wings and swooped down low. It dropped a bomb, which exploded, and shot at a hanging target with a machine gun. Then it buzzed past—so close that Gordon could see the red gleaming lights that were its eyes— looped around and back, and came in to land.

The director bowed and excused himself. When

he had gone inside, the count turned to Gordon.

"Gordon," he said in a grave voice, "I brought you here especially to see the dragonet because something important is happening. You know about the revolt in Ashby. It should not have succeeded. The reason it did is because somehow the rebels there obtained a weapon so large and powerful our Black Squads could not withstand it."

"A flying weapon," said Gordon. He remembered the creature he had seen flying over the citadel weeks before and wondered uneasily whether he should have said something. But his father was already continuing,

"This man, Lionel, has dared to call himself king of Ashby. He is wrong. We are the rulers of Ashby, Gordon, and we cannot tolerate people who defy us. Lionel, his friends, and his city will all be destroyed, and the dragonets are the weapons which will enable us to do it." The count looked lovingly at the tattered target that the dragonet had just shot down. "One day, when you are Black Count yourself, you will understand why these things must be done."

"Yes, Father." Gordon nodded. Inwardly, though, he felt some part of him grow cold. To cover his awkwardness, he asked, "Why are they called dragonets?"

"They're named after the creatures which were said to haunt these mountains long ago," said the count. "You've heard of Dragon's Downfall? Centuries ago, fire-breathing dragons were supposed to have fought there to the death. Of course, none of the tales are true."

"Oh." There was a deafening rattle below as the hangar door went down, and for a moment it was impossible to speak. Then Gordon heard the director's voice through a loudspeaker, announcing the end of the test. He and his father turned and went back into the factory.

Gordon was glad. He had not wanted to contradict his father, and he hadn't wanted the conversation to continue either. His thoughts were too confused. All he knew was that the thing he had seen from the turret bedroom on the cold night of his father's return now had a name.

It was a dragon.

The next morning, Gordon's father went away

again to the Ashby border to prepare for the invasion. Gordon went back to his normal routine of schoolwork and Boys' Squad. Every day, when the Black Squads had finished their drill, he and the other boys his age trooped out into the citadel courtyard for two hours of hard training in the freezing cold. When Gordon checked his orders he discovered, to his disgust, that today his troop was down for the obstacle course. It was something he particularly hated, partly because he wasn't much good at it, and partly because, as troop captain, he had to go first to show the rest of the boys how to do it.

"Fall in, troop. Atten—tion!" called Gordon, and the boys in his troop fell into line and snapped their feet together. While they stood watching, Gordon jogged over to the starting line. Two boys, Jacobsen and Harries, had already set up the course, and his heart sank when he saw how difficult it was. But there was no getting out of it. His lieutenant was already lifting the starter gun, and the timekeeper had his finger on the stopwatch.

"On your mark...go!"

Gordon ran straight for the hurdles. He

knocked over two of them, walked most of the way down the narrow timber balance beam before he fell off, and crawled through a tunnel of old truck tires. Ahead of him was a net and on the other side of it a water hazard, with a rope suspended over it. By now, he was starting to feel tired, but all he could think of was how embarrassing it would be if he couldn't get through the course before the bell rang.

Gordon came down from the net and ran for the water hazard. Too late to stop, he realized that the bar the rope was hanging from was set much farther back than it should have been. Summoning up his last ounce of energy, Gordon ran toward the rope and jumped, just catching it with both hands and swinging himself up off the ground.

What happened next he was never entirely able to explain. All he knew was that the rope lurched suddenly, swinging him in wild circles like a spider on its thread. Gordon felt a sharp pain in his left shoulder. Then there was an agonizing jerk, he felt himself falling toward the water, and there was nothing more.

chapter five

Angela

When Gordon woke up he was lying in bed with a bandage around his head. Two faces were staring down at him. Both were frowning, but when Gordon focused his eyes, one of them smiled.

"You've had a bad accident—" Angela began saying, but General Sark interrupted her.

"You've had an accident," he said brusquely. "A wrenched shoulder and mild concussion, according to the doctor here. If you'd fallen to the right you would have landed headfirst on the concrete and killed yourself." The general's pale eyes looked at Gordon disapprovingly. "Your father is not going to be very pleased when he hears what you've done."

"But I haven't done anything!" Gordon struggled to sit up. A pain flashed in his head, and he felt like he was about to throw up. Angela shook her head and made him lie down again.

"Don't move. You'll hurt yourself."

"Your Excellency should not make excuses," said General Sark. "You should have checked the course before you started it. The boys who set it up will be caned, of course. You will be expected to supervise their punishment yourself." The general nodded to Angela. "Take good care of him, Doctor. I will be back later to see how he is doing."

Gordon helplessly watched him go.

"It wasn't like that!" he said. "Nobody ever checks the courses before they run them. That's the job of the people who set it up. Honestly, it wasn't my fault!"

Angela came back from the door and sat beside his bed. "I'm sure it wasn't," she said. "But I wouldn't say anything, if I were you. Your friends are already getting a caning. If it came out that what happened was their fault, their punishment would be much, much worse."

They're not my friends. Gordon thought of Jacobsen and Harries, whom he didn't like very much, and opened his mouth to say so. But the words stopped in his throat. To tell the truth, to say that he hadn't any friends except Angela herself, seemed suddenly a very feeble thing to say.

As if she had somehow read his mind, Angela reached over and took his hand. Gordon held hers gratefully. Angela was always there when he needed her. He couldn't remember a time when she hadn't been. When he was a baby, in the coldest winter the Black Mountains had ever known, a terrible sickness had fallen on the Valley of the Citadel. It had killed his mother and hundreds of other people, and Gordon himself had been so ill none of his father's doctors could do anything to help him. Finally, somebody had remembered there was a doctor among the new batch of prisoners in the mines. The Black Count had sent for her, and Angela saved Gordon's life.

Ever since that day, Angela had been the count's own doctor. Some people said she was the only person who wasn't afraid to tell him the truth, and though she had never been able to persuade him to free the miners, occasionally, he even did what she suggested. Lots of people hated her, and many were afraid of her power, but the miners and poor people loved her. Gordon knew she still went down to the mining camps regularly to do what she could to help.

Now Angela glanced over her shoulder as if she were afraid someone was listening. She leaned close to Gordon and said in a low urgent voice, "Gordon, this is important. I want you to tell me exactly how your accident happened."

Gordon frowned, trying to remember. Then, suddenly it all came back: how the bar had been in the wrong place and the rope had broken. He told Angela everything, and a grave expression came over her face.

At last, when he finished, she said, "You're right, Gordon. The accident wasn't your fault. But I can't help wondering how the boys who laid out the course could have set it up like that unless they meant to."

Gordon's heart started beating faster. "What do you mean?" he asked.

"I mean," said Angela, "that someone has just tried to kill you. And unless you're very careful, they're likely to try again."

The crescent moon hung low over the horizon, and the stars gleamed in the cloudless sky. Standing on the battlements of Ashby Castle with King Lionel and Queen Evangeline, Lily thought she had never seen them shine so bright over Ashby Water before. She remembered the smoke pall from the grommet factory, and the orange fires that had once lit up the night sky, and shuddered. In the west, the moon dipped toward the distant mountains and disappeared.

"Do you think Queen Dragon will come?" asked Queen Evangeline.

"Well, she said she would," said Lily. "But she took an awful lot of persuading." All the Quench blood seemed to have drained out of her veins, and though she rubbed her right elbow surreptitiously through her flying jacket, the patch of dragon skin resolutely refused to tingle.

Now at last a dark shape like an enormous bat

appeared in the night sky. For a moment its giant wings blotted out the moonlight, and then it swooped down over their heads and circled back to land on the battlements. Lily heaved a sigh of relief and ran forward to greet her friend.

"Queen Dragon! I was starting to think you weren't coming!"

"I promised, didn't I?" Queen Dragon sniffed. Lily rubbed her cheek against her scaly crimson skin.

"I'm sorry," she said. "I guess I'm a little nervous, too." As she spoke, there was a sound of footsteps, and two more people appeared. It was Mr. Hartley and his assistant, Mr. Zouche.

"Your Majesties. Lily, if it's all right, I thought I'd come with you," said Mr. Hartley, and Lily saw to her surprise that he was dressed in a worn leather jacket and boots lined with sheepskin. He carried a leather flying cap and goggles, and Mr. Zouche held a neatly packed backpack with a frying pan dangling off the back. "It's a long way, and dangerous. I thought I might be useful."

"Hang on," said King Lionel. "This is Lily's quest, not yours. Anyway, who's going to look after Ashby Church while you're gone?"

"I will," growled Mr. Zouche, and Lionel and Evangeline looked alarmed. Captain Zouche had once been the Black Count's governor in Ashby. He had changed sides after his assistant, Miss Moldavia, had sent him to work in the grommet factory, and though Mr. Hartley had assured everyone he was quite reformed by the experience, no one was very comfortable when he was around. Lily was still rather scared of him. She had never forgotten the day when the captain and his Black Squad had burst into her house and dragged her off to the grommet factory to fight Queen Dragon.

"Wilibald will be fine," said Mr. Hartley, and he put his cap on his head and tied it firmly on. "Hand me the backpack, will you, Wilibald? Thanks."

"No," said Evangeline sharply, "stop right there. Nobody's said anything about wanting you on this quest. Don't you think it would be polite if you asked first? Lily? Queen Dragon? How do you feel about this?"

Lily looked at Queen Dragon, but her eyes were dark, and she seemed lost in some frightened world of her own. Lily felt a pang of fear. Until now, with Queen Dragon at her side, she had always felt safe. But this terror of Dragon's Downfall was something new. For the first time, Lily could not help thinking it might be good to have someone else along, too.

"Thank you, Mr. Hartley. Queen Dragon and I would be glad to have you," she said gratefully, and Mr. Hartley smiled. He tied his backpack alongside Lily's on the strap around Queen Dragon's neck, and reached down to give her a leg up. A few minutes later, after everyone had said good-bye, Queen Dragon took flight and soared away toward the west.

Crystal Bright was sulking, and the whole of Ashby Castle knew it. Ever since the council meeting, she had made herself thoroughly obnoxious to everyone. She threw tantrums, broke things, slapped the servants, and, at last, locked herself in her bedroom. For days, the sound of her yells and kicks had resounded through the castle, but Evangeline had told everyone to ignore her, and eventually her tantrum had run out of steam.

Since then, nobody had seen her. They'd heard her, though, playing her favorite single over and over again at top volume. And while nobody minded hearing Sandy Shaw sing "Puppet on a String" once or even twice, by the four hundred and seventy-ninth time, it was starting to become a strain.

"Doesn't she ever get sick of listening to it?" asked Lionel over dinner. The single reached the end, and there was a pause as the automatic replay kicked in.

Evangeline thoughtfully bit into her sausage. "Nobody's as stubborn as Mother when she puts her mind to it. She's just trying to wear us down. The only thing to do is to pretend she isn't there. Besides, do you want to tell her to turn it off?"

Lionel didn't. Neither did anyone else, and since all the servants loathed her, Crystal was left to her own devices. Nobody even bothered to call her down for meals. Since her room was stuffed with chocolates, biscuits, canned pâté, and bottled caviar, this hardly mattered. Crystal was already eating better than practically anybody else in Ashby.

But on the morning after Lily and Queen Dragon's departure, something happened. Crystal's single stuck.

Evangeline was the first to notice it. She sat up in bed, woken up by the racket, and then poked her husband in the ribs.

"Lionel. Listen."

Lionel opened his eyes. Sure enough, in the opposite bedroom, Sandy Shaw sounded as if she had a bad case of hiccups. He and Evangeline looked at each other and threw back the bedclothes. They jumped out of bed and ran across the corridor to Crystal's room.

"Mother?" called Evangeline. *Mother!*"

There was no reply. Evangeline went back to the royal bedroom and fetched the scepter from its stand at the foot of the bed. Once, the Ashby scepter had been silver with a ruby-studded head. Unfortunately, that one had been lost when the Black Count invaded, and Lionel had been obliged to make do with one of the grommet factory railings, painted gold. Being iron, it was extremely strong. When Evangeline brought it down with all her strength on Crystal's door, the lock shattered and the record player fell with a smash onto the floor.

"Mother? Are you in there?" Evangeline tried peering through the hole in the door, then wriggled her hand through to the other side and unbolted it. "Oh no!" she gasped out loud.

The room inside was empty. Crystal had disappeared.

MISSING PERSON
REWARD

Mrs Crystal Bright
Small plump woman with
sharp-looking teeth and
Purple streaked hair.
Last seen around Ashby
Castle...

chapter six

Tina's Bombshell

Queen Dragon flew on steadily through the
night, steering herself westward by the stars.
Lily and Mr. Hartley did not say much. It was
hard to talk with the sound of the wind and
Queen Dragon's wingstrokes filling their ears, and
anyway, neither of them had very much to say.
From time to time they flew over a farmhouse
with twinkling lights, roads lit by streetlamps, and
small towns that Queen Dragon knew by name.
But mostly there was nothing to look at but the
stars, and then the clouds closed in, and there was
nothing to see at all.

Dawn came hours later in a sullen red band around the eastern horizon, and Queen Dragon veered to the north. Despite the sunlight and the dragon's warmth beneath them, it started to get horribly cold. Lily adjusted her goggles and wrapped her scarves and fireproof cape more tightly around her face. Her breath had formed ice crystals in the folds of the material, and it crackled when she touched it. Her hands ached in their thick leather gauntlets, and her booted feet were so numb she could hardly feel them at all. The daylight grew gradually brighter, and then, through a brief gap in the clouds, she saw a dark smudge ahead.

"Look." She pointed. "The Black Mountains."

Mr. Hartley followed her gaze. "So they are," he said softly, and did not utter another word until they landed above the pass.

Lionel and Evangeline sat together gloomily in the Royal Council chamber. On the table was a freshly printed poster with a picture of Crystal on it. The caption above the photo read **MISSING**

PERSON: REWARD Underneath it was Crystal's name, a description, and the details of her disappearance.

"I hope Mother never sees this," said Evangeline. "She's bound to get offended and say the reward money is too small."

"Too bad," said Lionel. "It's all we can afford, and anyway, I'm sure it's not going to work. If you ask me, she's either been kidnapped or she's run away. If she's run away, we'll get a postcard from some fancy resort and a heap of bills; and if she's been kidnapped, we'll get a ransom note." He sighed. "Either way, I don't think the treasury can stand it."

"Perhaps she'll come back of her own accord," said Evangeline hopefully.

Lionel shrugged. Evangeline folded up the poster and bit her lip. To Lionel, Crystal's disappearance was just another thing to worry about. But Crystal was her mother, and, whatever other people thought, she still loved her. It was hard not to fear that something truly bad had gone wrong.

Someone knocked on the door. Evangeline put away the poster.

"Come in!"

The door opened, and Mr. Zouche entered the room. With him was a small, mouse-brown girl with mouse-brown hair, neat features, and a worried expression. She was wearing a drab blue dress and carried a crumpled paper bag.

"Your Majesties," growled Mr. Zouche, "this is Tina. She works in the church office. Says she's got something important to tell you, but she won't let me know what it is."

"That's not true," said Tina indignantly. "I never said I wouldn't tell you. I just said, I thought Their Majesties ought to be told first."

"That's quite all right, Tina," said King Lionel kindly. "Please sit down. Her Majesty and I would be interested to hear what you've come to say."

"Thank you, Your Majesty." Tina gave a tiny sniff and pulled up a chair. She opened the paper bag and produced a small black book, a bit like a diary, with a loop on the cover for a pencil. Tina pulled out the pencil and started flipping through the pages.

"Hey!" Zouche was outraged. "That's Mr. Hartley's private notebook! What are you doing with it, you little creep?"

"I am not a creep! I thought it was an address book until I opened it," Tina flared. She handed the book to King Lionel and stabbed at the page with her finger. "Look, Your Majesty. It's there in black and white. Dates, times, everything. Mr. Hartley has been going back and forth to the Black Empire for years. He's a spy for the Black Count!"

Evangeline gasped.

"A spy!" Mr. Zouche roared. "What are you talking about, girl? Mr. Hartley? A spy!"

King Lionel winced. "Wilibald, please be quiet." He rifled through the notebook's pages, and his face started looking grim.

"I will not be quiet! Utter bosh and nonsense!" bawled Mr. Zouche. His face was getting redder and redder with every moment.

"It's not bosh and nonsense! It's the truth!" retorted Tina.

"If I say it's bosh, it is bosh! As if the king and queen would believe a word you'd say, you grubby little grommeteer!"

Tina jumped to her feet. "Don't you call me a grommeteer, you fat pig! Who'd believe you, anyway? You worked for the Black Count for years and made everyone's life miserable. Then just because you were clever enough to change sides at the last moment, you think it gives you the right to keep telling us what to do. Well, you're wrong! Things have changed here. I've never been so happy in my life since King Lionel came back. I hate the Black Count. And I'll do whatever it takes to stop him coming back, even if it means handing Mr. Hartley over to the king!" With that, she burst into tears and ran out.

The throne room was perfectly silent. Evangeline and Lionel sat looking at each other, and then Evangeline took the notebook from Lionel and started leafing through its pages. The sides of her mouth slowly turned down. Like everybody else, Evangeline trusted and liked Mr. Hartley. Like Lionel, she had thought he was a good, kind person. But the notebook in her hands told a different story.

"I don't believe her," said Mr. Zouche. "There has to have been a mistake."

"I'm sorry, Wilibald," said Lionel, "but I think Tina's got a point. Look at the notebook. All those visits to the Black Mountains—what legitimate reason could he have for going there?"

"I don't need to look at the notebook," said Mr. Zouche. "I know Mr. Hartley wouldn't betray us. There has to be another explanation."

"But what can it be, Wilibald?" asked Evangeline. "As Tina says, it's here in black and white. Ever since the count first invaded Ashby, Mr. Hartley has been to the Black Mountains over and over again. And look here: he actually writes 'saw the Black Count today.' What more proof do you need?"

"I don't care. There's still a mistake," said Zouche stubbornly. "Your Majesties, please listen to me. I know hardly anybody in Ashby likes me. Nobody trusts me because I used to work for the Black Count. Well, maybe they're right. I did work for the count, I was even proud of it. I was a bad person, and a lot of people would say I still am. But Mr. Hartley was different. He was the only person in Ashby who believed in me. If it hadn't been for him, I would never have had the courage to change. So because he spoke up for me, I'm going to do the same for him. I swear, Mr. Hartley is not a spy. Remember, I was working for the count myself. I know I'm telling you the truth."

"Thank you, Wilibald," said Lionel. "I appreciate what you have told me. You may leave now."

Mr. Zouche stood up. He opened his mouth as if he would have liked to say something further. Then he changed his mind, clicked his heels, and left the room.

There was a long silence. At last, King Lionel lifted his head.

"He's got a point, you know. He was in charge here for many years."

Evangeline shook her head sadly. "He means well," she said. "In fact, I'm sure he thinks he's telling the truth. But the fact is, even though Zouche was supposed to be in charge, there was a lot he didn't know. Miss Moldavia almost made herself queen of Ashby right under his nose, and he didn't even guess what she was doing. And besides, it was always Miss Moldavia the spies reported to. I know, because she tried to make me one."

"I suppose you're right," said Lionel. "But it still seems so unreal. You know, Miss Moldavia had Mr. Hartley thrown into prison. She tried to force him into marrying her to me so she could become queen, but he refused. I suppose if he was loyal to the Black Count he would still have done that, but all the same . . . I just cannot believe he's a spy."

"Successful spies are always the most unlikely people," said Evangeline bleakly. "And the worst of it is that Mr. Hartley has been to all the Royal Council meetings since your coronation. He knows every single thing we've been planning."

"No," said Lionel. "That's not the worst of it. The worst of it is that we've just sent him off with Lily and Queen Dragon to the Black Mountains. They don't know any of this. And if Tina's right—if the notebook is right, and Mr. Hartley is working for the Black Empire—then we've just sent both of them into a trap."

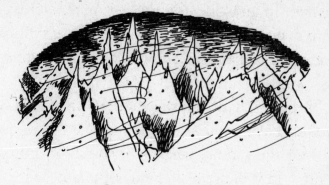

chapter seven

In the Black Mountains

Because of his accident, Gordon had been excused from training with the Boys' Squad. But he could not get out of Jacobsen and Harries's caning, and the next day he and the rest of his troop reported to the citadel's punishment block to watch. While everyone else stood to attention, Gordon sat alone on a platform at the front of the room. The two prisoners were brought out and caned ten hard strokes on each hand. Jacobsen cried and got five more. Afterward, on the way out, Gordon wished he could have said sorry. But there was no chance of that. In any case, the look of pure, murderous hatred on Harries's face, as he held his bruised fingers in a basin of snow, would have stopped the words in his throat.

Nobody had ever caned Gordon. They wouldn't dare.

After the caning, when he was safe in his own room and it didn't matter how much he trembled and shook, it occurred to Gordon that none of the other boys in the troop had felt sorry for him at all. Even though he had done nothing wrong; even though Jacobsen and Harries had deliberately set up the obstacle course so he would fall and hurt himself; even though he could have been killed, every other boy in the room had been on their side, not his. A few sucked up to him, but none of them really liked him. In fact, Gordon realized, they hated him.

But my father is the count! thought Gordon indignantly. *They've no right to hate me. I can't help who I am.* For a while he brooded on this, and then it all got too hard and unfair. He got a bar of chocolate out of his drawer, peeled off the wrapper, and went over and sat looking out of the window instead.

The sky was low, and a few snowflakes were fluttering down again. Another storm was brewing, but the Black Squads were doing drill as usual in the castle courtyard, marching up and down and standing to attention in the snow. Gordon sucked the caramel filling out of his chocolate. A few minutes went by, and he saw Angela trudging back in her snowshoes from the miners' camp. She had been down there all morning, delivering a baby, and Gordon wondered whether it had been a boy or a girl. If it was a boy, it would be taken from its mother and sent to the Black Squad nursery so it could become a soldier. For this reason he knew Angela always hoped for baby girls, and somehow today this made him crosser than ever.

Angela disappeared inside, and Gordon turned back to the Black Squads. The snow was starting to fall more heavily now, and the wind was rising, but the squads kept on marching back and forth through the showers of snowflakes. Normally by now the drill should have finished, but they showed no signs of stopping. Something or someone was keeping them out there, long past the time when the exercise should have been over.

Gordon looked toward the officers and suddenly he recognized a face that should not have been there. General Sark was standing in his greatcoat, drilling the troops himself. Gordon could not understand what he was doing, but it made him strangely afraid. The general lifted his face to his turret, and it seemed to Gordon that he was staring at him where he sat in his bedroom window. Then the snow started coming down in earnest, and he could see no more.

High above the citadel, on the peak of Dragon's Neck, Lily, Mr. Hartley, and Queen Dragon were also battening down against the storm. Mr. Hartley had pointed out a cave that was big enough to take the three of them, and together they had set up camp and lit their stove. Now Mr. Hartley was making hot chocolate from melted snow, cocoa, and milk powder, and Lily was standing in the freezing cold trying to talk Queen Dragon into going on with their mission.

"What are you so frightened of?" she shouted, rather louder than she had intended. It was hard to make herself heard over the roar of the storm. But Queen Dragon just shook her head and refused to say anything. In the end, Lily gave up.

"Queen Dragon won't fly us into Dragon's Downfall," she reported to Mr. Hartley in a troubled voice. "She says it's a bad place."

"She's probably right," said Mr. Hartley. "The Black Mountains are full of unhappy memories." He looked around the cave. "You know, I don't think this is a natural cave. It's an old mine. The people who dug it would have been slaves, brought from one of the conquered kingdoms of the Black Empire. Maybe they even came from Ashby."

"You mean, there are slaves from Ashby in these mountains?" Lily was shocked.

"Oh, yes," said Mr. Hartley. "In fact, somebody very dear to me was taken prisoner, long ago in the Siege of Ashby. Nobody has seen her since." A look of faraway sadness came into his eyes and Lily thought it best not to ask any more questions.

Shortly after lunch, the snowstorm finally cleared. Lily and Mr. Hartley packed up their tent, sleeping bags, and enough provisions for two days in the mountains. Queen Dragon promised to look after the rest of their belongings while they were gone. Before they left, she made Lily practice the Dragons' Cry of Summoning. This was a special call she had taught her during their winter together on Skansey, which brought assistance to any dragon in distress.

"Do take care, Lily," she said anxiously. "I have such a bad feeling about this."

"I'll be careful," Lily promised her. "And I'll remember the Cry of Summoning, too." She and Mr. Hartley waved good-bye and shouldered their backpacks. Then, with a cheery wave, they set off down the hill in the direction of Dragon's Downfall.

By the time dinner arrived, Gordon was almost certain something was wrong in the citadel. Maybe it was the enthusiastic way the Black Squad soldiers marched around the battlements, or the extra guards who suddenly appeared at the checkpoints. Or it could have been the strange bustle of activity in the citadel cellars. On the other hand, it might just have been that his dinner was late and he was cross. Gordon had asked for a hamburger with salad and an ice cream sundae, but instead the kitchen sent up a slice of frozen pizza, barely heated, and no dessert at all.

"You shouldn't complain, Gordon. Some people have nothing to eat," said Angela sharply when he grumbled about it. She was sitting with him in his turret, knitting a long white scarf out of knobbly wool. Normally when Angela spoke like this, it made Gordon feel ashamed. Tonight, it just made him angry.

"I don't care about other people."

"Then you should. One day, when your father is dead and you're in charge of the Black Empire, you'll have to look after them."

"Like my father does?" said Gordon. At this, Angela dropped a stitch and did not look up. Gordon felt glad. Unlike Angela, who was always trying to help, he knew his father didn't really care about other people. It didn't matter whether they loved or hated him, as long as they obeyed him. Gordon remembered how miserable he had felt after the caning, and suddenly found himself longing to be like that, too. Perhaps, he thought, it was this that made his father so strong.

"My father ought to come back to the citadel," he said suddenly. "Something peculiar's happening; he needs to be here. But all he can think of is invading Ashby."

Angela did not reply. She found the stitch she had dropped, knitted it up, and continued to the end of the row. Gordon started to feel uncomfortable. Had he said something he shouldn't? He looked again, and realized from the droop of Angela's shoulders, from the dejected way she was sitting, that tonight she was not disapproving, but intensely sad. And at that moment he remembered something she had once told him, something he had almost completely forgotten. Angela herself had come from a town called Ashby Water.

"Do you mind?" he blurted out suddenly. "I mean, it's a long time since you lived in Ashby. It was before I was born. You must have almost forgotten it."

Angela put her knitting down in her lap. She rubbed her right eye with the back of her hand, and Gordon saw it came away wet.

"Of course I haven't forgotten it," she said.

"Ashby is my home. I think about it every day of my life. And I worry about what will happen. If there's an invasion, it will be terrible."

"There *will* be an invasion," said Gordon. "My father's planning it. And anyway, you shouldn't be sorry for those people. They fought the Black Squads and knocked down the grommet factory, and they crowned their own king in place of my father. They deserve to be invaded."

"Do they really, though?" said Angela. "You've never been in an invasion, Gordon. I have. I stood on the battlements of Ashby Castle during the Siege ten years ago. I saw King Alwyn the Last and Godfrey Quench fall into a moat full of flames, and then I saw my husband disappear into the fire, too, trying to save their lives. I watched my friends be taken prisoner; I saw people starve. And then I was taken away as a slave. I nearly died in the mines the first winter that I came here. Did I deserve that just because I was born in Ashby Water? Does anyone?"

"Yes," said Gordon in a small voice. "They do."

"If you say so, Gordon," said Angela wearily, and somehow, the fact that she did not even care enough to argue with him made Gordon worried enough to finally ask the question on the tip of his tongue.

"You don't want to leave, do you?" he asked. Angela did not reply, and he said urgently, "Promise me, Angela. Promise you'll stay with me."

Angela paused. "I promise I'll always love you, Gordon," she said, and she put her arm around him and held him close. In his heart, Gordon knew this was not the promise he had asked for. But it was easier to persuade himself that this was what Angela had meant.

Because of their late start, Lily and Mr. Hartley had not gone far before the sun started dropping over the mountain. They decided to stop for the night and pitched their tent in a little gully sloping down toward the valley floor.

Even though she was very tired and her sleeping bag was warm and cozy, Lily found it hard to get to sleep. In Ashby it never snowed, so she wasn't used to the cold, and Mr. Hartley kept muttering in his sleep as if he was having a bad dream. Then she started thinking about Dragon's Downfall. Suppose Queen Dragon was right, and there was something terrible waiting for them there? And yet somehow, both her grandmother and Matilda Drakescourge had managed to bring the blue lily back to Ashby. Lily decided they must have been very determined people.

At last she dropped off and woke soon after dawn with the scent of breakfast in her nostrils. Mr. Hartley was up, and sausages, bacon, and eggs were sizzling in a small frying pan. Lily's stomach rumbled. She pulled her boots and cloak on and scrambled out of the tent.

"Yum," she said. "How long before it's ready?"

"A few minutes," said Mr. Hartley. "While it's cooking, shall we go up onto that ridge? We should be able to get a good view of where we're headed."

Together they set off up the slope, leaving the breakfast frying in its pan. From the ridge they could see fields of snow and ice stretching away into the valley of Dragon's Downfall. Jagged black rocks poked up out of the whiteness like broken teeth, and in the distance they could hear water gushing in some wild torrent. It did not look like a very enticing prospect.

"I think Queen Dragon might be right," Lily began, but a loud roar from down the slope cut off her words. There was a terrible crash from the camp below them, and the green tent suddenly billowed upward like a jellyfish and collapsed.

"Something's attacked the camp!" Lily started running wildly back down the slope. At the gully's bottom she skidded to a halt, a look of absolute horror on her face. Their campsite was in ruins, and a huge brown bear was standing in the midst of it, snarling, with a string of half-cooked sausages in its paw.

chapter eight

The Golden Child

M r. Hartley grabbed Lily's shoulder and pulled
her behind a rock. "Stand very still," he said.

Lily froze. The bear had not yet seen them, but
it was sniffing the air with the sort of concentration
that made her sure it had caught their scent.

Their stove had been knocked over on the
snow and had gone out. The frying pan lay a
little distance away, and Lily guessed the bear had
already eaten the bacon and eggs. As she watched,
it picked up her sleeping bag and shook it
around. Then it dropped to all fours and started
nosing among their provisions.

The bear pulled the last remaining string of raw sausages from Lily's backpack and ate them thoughtfully. It found the biscuits and the apples she had brought from Skansey and ate them, too, and it ripped open their tea packet and scattered the leaves over the snow. Finally it dragged at the ruined tent again with its paws. Lily winced as she heard its great claws ripping through the material. There was a lot of growling and snuffling before it stood up again.

"I think it's going," she whispered.

Mr. Hartley put his finger to his lips.

The bear stood very still, listening. It turned and looked directly at the rock where Lily and Mr. Hartley were crouching. Lily caught her breath. She clung to the rock so hard that it hurt her fingers through her gloves. Then, after what seemed like an eternity, the bear dropped down and lumbered away in the opposite direction.

Lily let go of the rock. She would have run straight down to their campsite, but Mr. Hartley held her back. Together they waited, growing colder and colder as the minutes passed. But the bear did not return, and after about ten minutes had gone by, they went down the gully to their ruined camp.

"What a mess!" Lily exclaimed.

"Has it left us any food at all?" asked Mr. Hartley.

Lily looked sadly at the spilled provisions. "A couple of cans of baked beans." Her tummy rumbled as she said it. Mr. Hartley picked up half an apple, looked at the bear's teeth marks, and threw it away.

"Well, at least it couldn't open the cans," he said.

"I hate baked beans," said Lily in a woebegone voice.

"Nonsense. You'll enjoy anything if you're hungry enough. Let's light the stove again, and we'll have those tins warmed up in a second."

Mr. Hartley set busily to work. While he warmed the beans, Lily sorted through the remains of the tent. She found a chocolate bar that the bear had somehow missed, and by the time the beans were ready she felt rather better. Strangely enough, Mr. Hartley was right. Her hunger really did make the baked beans taste all right, cooked in their cans with a sort of metallic tang to flavor them. And since Mr. Hartley nobly let her eat the entire chocolate bar, by the end of the meal she was feeling much more her usual Quench-like self.

"What next?" she asked, wiping the tomato sauce off her mouth. "Should we go back to Queen Dragon?"

"It's really up to you, Lily," said Mr. Hartley. "You're the one in charge of the quest. What do you think?"

"Well...I think we should keep on with the mission," said Lily. The chocolate had made her feel brave, and besides, the scales on her elbow were tingling faintly. While that sometimes meant danger ahead, it was also often a good sign.

"Good," said Mr. Hartley. "I think so, too. Let's leave the tent and sleeping bags here. We'll need to get back to Queen Dragon by nightfall, so there's no point in carrying them with us."

While Mr. Hartley buried their trash, Lily found her map and the copy of Matilda's diary, untouched in the metal cylinder where she kept her telescope. She put them into her backpack, along with her matches and compass, and slung it over her shoulders. Then, having put on their snowshoes, they set off once more into the white and silent valley.

"Your father has sent a message by courier bird," said General Sark. "He says he wants you to go out on patrol with the Black Squads."

Gordon looked up from his project on the Black Mountains' iron deposits. His first thought was how great it would be to get outside again after his accident. Then he remembered how Angela had told him to be careful and started wondering what this was about.

"Did my father send me a letter?" he asked suspiciously.

"No." Gordon could almost see the dislike in the general's pale green eyes. "Your father is busy preparing for the Ashby Invasion. He hasn't time to write to you."

"I see," said Gordon. His heart started thumping uncomfortably, for he knew that, whatever his father was doing, however busy he was, he always found time to drop Gordon a note. General Sark was lying. Gordon was sure he wanted to get him out of the way, but he had no idea why.

"All right then, can I read your orders?" he asked rudely.

This time there was no mistaking the flash of anger in Sark's eyes. "No, you may not," he said. "They were sent to me, not you. Get your coat on, Gordon. There's a snow patrol going out in about fifteen minutes. For your own sake, I think you'd better be on it."

Shortly before midday, the sound of running water became a roar somewhere ahead. Lily, who had seen waterfalls on her visit to the Singing Wood, decided there must be a big one quite nearby. There was also another sound: an eerie snapping, popping, dripping she could not immediately place.

"It's spring in these mountains," explained Mr. Hartley. "The ice is melting. Though, of course, it's so cold here the snow never goes away completely."

Lily shuddered. "Imagine living in a place like this."

"Imagine," agreed Mr. Hartley. "Nothing grows here, Lily. There's nothing in the Black Mountains but snow and ice, and iron for making weapons. Anything the men and women of these mountains need to live—food, clothes, fuel—they have to get from somewhere else. That's why the counts started building up the Black Empire, so long ago. They did it just to survive."

"How do you know all this?" asked Lily curiously.

"I don't really know that much," said Mr. Hartley. "I've just been here a few times, looking for someone." He changed the subject. "Look, here we are on the edge of the map. Dragon's Downfall is just ahead. We'd better go carefully."

The two friends continued on for a short distance. Lily let her eyes roam ahead. The terrain was steep and covered with snow, but it seemed no more dangerous than anything else they had encountered so far. Then her eyes caught sight of something jutting out of the snow.

"Look!" She pointed. "That rock, over there!

It's got a hole through it, just like the one Matilda drew in her journal!"

They pressed on and reached the rock after a few minutes of brisk walking. Lily could see at once it was the one Matilda had drawn. It was very tall and black with rough sloping sides and a point on the top. The hole had smooth sides and went right through.

"I wonder who put it there?" Lily peeped into the hole. It looked just big enough for her to crawl through, and she poked her head and shoulders into it. A flash of blue showed at the other end. Excited, Lily started to wriggle into the gap. Mr. Hartley grabbed her collar and pulled her back.

"Better not," he said. "Crawl in there, Lily, and you never know where you might end up. Too many people have already gone missing in this valley. We mustn't take any chances."

"Sorry." Lily shook her head. "You know, for a moment, I had a really weird feeling. Like I had to go through that hole to finish the quest. I wonder where it came from?"

"I don't know, but you can be sure, from nowhere good," said Mr. Hartley. "Queen Dragon is right when she says this valley is a dangerous place. We have to remember our mission and not get carried away by feelings."

Lily picked up their backpack, and they walked carefully around the stone.

Now the ground started to slope down steeply, and ahead they could see the edge of a cliff. The sound Lily had thought was a waterfall grew louder and louder, and when she walked over to the brink, she could see a river smashing and boiling its way through forests of sharp, gray rocks in the valley far below. The dizzying heights made Lily feel sick and frightened, but somehow excited, too. Even where she stood, high above the water, the icy spray drifted up and spattered her face.

"Wow!" she said. "Look at the rocks! And down there—I can see something glistening. It's a person—no, it's a statue made of gold!" Lily's voice peaked, and she reached for her telescope. Halfway down the cliff, on a jutting-out ledge of rock, stood a statue of a boy in a cloak. The golden folds were so lifelike they almost looked as if they were billowing in the wind, and as the eyepiece of the telescope wobbled in Lily's frozen fingers, he seemed to look up at her and smile.

Suddenly, the Golden Child beckoned. Lily got such a shock she dropped the telescope. Behind her, she could hear Mr. Hartley yelling her name, but his voice seemed a long way off. The Golden Child smiled at her, telling her to come down the cliff. Mr. Hartley was still yelling, telling her to think of Lionel and Ashby and the blue lily, but Lily could hardly hear any of it, and if she had, she wouldn't have paid any attention. She dropped to her knees and started swinging her legs over the cliff.

"Lily!" shouted Mr. Hartley. "Stop! Think of Queen Dragon!" And somehow, through the fuzz in her brain, Lily remembered Queen Dragon and heard a dragonish voice in her head, telling her to be careful. The Golden Child screamed with rage, and Queen Dragon roared; for a moment the two voices fought in Lily's head, each struggling to be heard over the other. Then the roar of the dragon drowned out the shrill crying of the boy, and at once Lily knew Queen Dragon was right, that Dragon's Downfall was a bad place and that the people who listened to the Golden Child were the ones who never returned.

"It's all right, Queen Dragon!" she yelled. "I hear you!"

Immediately, the voices in her head stopped calling and everything went deathly still.

Lily lay in the snow on the edge of the cliff. Below her, the Golden Child stood winking in the sunlight. It was just a statue. But around it, lying in the open air, she could now see the bleached skeletons of the travelers who hadn't made it, scattered all the way down the cliff to the river below.

"Are you all right, Lily?" asked Mr. Hartley. He was sitting a little way away, looking white-faced and sick.

"I think so," said Lily shakily. "It was calling me to jump off."

"And me," said Mr. Hartley. "I would have done it, too, if I hadn't thought of someone very special. Remembering her gave me the strength to keep hanging on." Suddenly he laughed. "Look, Lily," he said. "We almost missed it. The blue lily!" He pointed, and Lily caught sight of a gleam of blue in the snow.

"The blue lily!" Lily wriggled forward across the snow. She brought her trowel out of her pocket and started to dig around the base of the plant. The blue flower trembled on its stalk. Lily worked her fingers into the hole, trying to get at the roots. Then, just as the bulb came free, there was a horrible lurch and the cliff started moving underneath her.

Lily felt herself slipping toward the edge. She yelled, her head and shoulders dangling in midair, and then something pulled her up short. Mr. Hartley had grabbed her feet and pulled her back, just in time.

Lily lay, panting on the snow, the precious bulb clutched tightly in her hand. Mr. Hartley helped her to her feet.

"Come on," he said. "We've been here too long already. It's time to get back to Queen Dragon."

The journey back was very tiring. Even if they hadn't been walking on snow, it was all uphill and still a long way, and Lily was afraid they might get lost in the alien whiteness. She was also starting to feel very hungry, and she realized that, unless they made it back to the cave and

Queen Dragon by nightfall, there was no chance of any dinner. The prospect made her feel quite faint.

At last, late in the afternoon, they rounded the bend that led into the gully where their camp had been. Lily saw the green of their fallen tent, lying dark against the snow, and summoned up a last burst of energy. When they reached the camp, she stopped in amazement.

"Someone else has been here!" she exclaimed. "There are footprints in the snow."

Her words were cut off by the purring of a motor. Lily looked up and saw a sleek black snowmobile heading down the upper reaches of the gully. Behind the rocks where they had sheltered from the bear, dark human shapes moved against the snow.

"Black Squads!" Lily and Mr. Hartley started to run, but there was no time to get away. The snowmobile stopped a little distance away and half a dozen soldiers in dark anoraks and fur-lined hats jumped down and ran toward them.

"Put your hands in the air," said a muffled voice, and the speaker jumped down from the snowmobile and walked toward them.

"Why, you're only a girl!" he said in surprise as he neared them. Lily realized in turn that the boy who spoke was hardly older than herself. He had dark hair and a pale face, and there was a white bandage on his forehead. Despite this, he was wearing a uniform with a lot of gold braid on it and looked as if he was important. Lily tried to look him in the face, but she was tired and hungry and all her Quench-like qualities seemed to have fled. Even the expression in his eyes made her feel afraid.

"Who are you?" said the boy. "What are you doing in these mountains?"

Though it took all her courage, Lily did not answer. Nor did Mr. Hartley. The boy looked at them a moment longer, then made an impatient gesture with his hand.

"Handcuff them together," said Gordon, "and put them in the back. I'm sure they'll be more helpful back at the citadel."

chapter nine

The Black Citadel

As soon as they reached the Black Citadel, Lily and Mr. Hartley were separated. Lily, who had tried hard not to feel terrified when the snowmobile drove through the huge black gates, was locked alone in a small, windowless room. There was no furniture in it, not even a chair, and it was hardly bigger than a cupboard. Lily felt her way into a darkened corner, crouched with her arms around her knees, and miserably closed her eyes tight shut.

After about ten minutes the door opened and the boy who had been on the snowmobile came into the room. He was carrying Lily's backpack and had taken off his coat with the braid on it, but the uniform he wore still looked terribly important. Lily thought he had the coldest eyes she had ever seen.

"What's your name, girl?" he asked.

Lily decided to tell the truth. "I'm Lily."

"Lily what?"

"Lily—Cornstalk."

"All right, Lily Cornstalk. You've got some explaining to do. What were you doing in that gully?"

"We were just on our way back from Dragon's Downfall."

"Dragon's Downfall? Surely you don't expect me to believe that. Nobody goes down there and comes back alive."

Lily did not reply. Partly, she was too scared, and partly she realized she had already said the wrong thing. Instead, she sat on the floor and looked at the boy, waiting for him to speak, until he started to get restless and uncomfortable.

"You're lying," he said. "And you're lying to the wrong person. Do you know who I am? My name is Gordon. My father is the Black Count.

If you don't tell me the truth, I can have you sent to the mines for the rest of your life."

"But I am telling you the truth," said Lily. "Honestly, I am."

"All right. Suppose you are," said Gordon. "Why were you in Dragon's Downfall, and what were you doing?"

"I was collecting flowers," said Lily.

Gordon's face went slowly red. "Stop making fun of me!" he yelled. "Who do you think I am? Nobody talks to me like that. I'll speak to my father and have you locked up!"

"But I'm already locked up," Lily pointed out.

It was the wrong thing to say. Gordon stamped his foot and started having the worst temper tantrum Lily had ever seen in her life. He shouted and raved, telling Lily she was a creep and a liar and a traitor, and that he would have her sent to the deepest shaft in the worst mine in the entire Black Empire. Lily said nothing. The blue lily was still in her pocket. Its scent floated out to her, rich and strong and overpoweringly beautiful. It made her feel calm somehow, while Gordon just got more and more worked up.

"Listen," he said at last, when he'd run out of

things to say and there was nothing left to do but calm down again. "There's no point in lying to me. You'll have to tell the truth eventually. It'll only make things worse for you in the end."

"But I'm not lying," Lily insisted. "Mr. Hartley and I are... plant collectors. We went down into the valley looking for rare flowers. Oh, and we met a bear on the way. It ate our breakfast and tore down our tent. You can go back and check if you want to."

"Stop it!" Gordon shouted. "Stop it! Listen to me, Lily Cornstalk. Nobody, except one man, has ever been down into Dragon's Downfall and come back alive. That was more than a hundred years ago, and he went stark raving mad. The Black Counts have spent centuries trying to discover what it is down there that kills people, but nobody's ever been able to find out. Why? Because nobody but a loony's ever come back, do you hear me? Nobody!"

Suddenly Gordon's words were cut off. A bell had started tolling deep in the citadel. Its heavy stroke echoed hollowly down the corridors and sent shivers through the concrete walls of Lily's cell; it struck up through the floor and sent vibrations shuddering through her body. Abruptly, Gordon's expression changed. He no longer looked angry, but shocked and frightened instead.

"What is it?" said Lily. "What's happening?"

Gordon stared at her. "It's the Great Bell," he said. "It hasn't been rung in over fifty years. It means there's been an attack on the citadel."

"An attack—" For the second time they were interrupted, this time by swift footsteps in the corridor. Gordon threw himself at the door and Lily caught a brief glimpse of a plump woman in a fur coat. But it was already too late. The light went out. The cell door slammed shut, and there was the sound of a key turning in the lock.

They were trapped.

"What do you mean, a dragon?" said General Sark irritably. He was standing in the window of Gordon's turret, watching his handpicked Black Squads round up the last of the Black Count's supporters. In a moment he would go out and take control of the Black Empire. It was his great moment of triumph, planned in secret for years, and now *she* was trying to spoil it. "You don't mean the Dragon of Ashby, do you? And anyway, who's this Lily Quench?"

"Someone you don't want to tangle with," said Crystal Bright. She sat on Gordon's desk, swinging her elegantly booted legs back and forth. Her hands were tucked into the sleeves of her long fur coat, for the window was open and it was very cold. "Sark, I've been sending you letters for years, telling you what was happening. Didn't you read any of them? I'm telling you, you've got Lily Quench down in that dungeon of yours. *The* Lily Quench. The Lily Quench who went to the Singing Wood and led the revolt that put my worm of a son-in-law on his unrightful throne."

"So you've said. Already. Several times," Sark retorted. "Look here, Ruby, er, Crystal. All that stuff about Ashby and the dragon was really useful. It's kept the count down on the border and out of my way for months, and I'm really grateful to you. But just now I've got an empire to conquer, the count's still loose, and that repellent boy Gordon is roaming around the citadel—"

"Oh. Really?" Crystal smiled secretively.

"—and I don't know where he is," finished Sark. "The patrol captain was supposed to keep him out there until everything was over and bring him back as a hostage, but apparently they took some prisoners and the silly idiot came back early."

"Sark, cutie," said Crystal, "cut to the point. We've got a deal. You become emperor of the Black Empire, I become the empress and queen of Ashby. No," she corrected herself, "Queen Mother. Evangeline can still be queen, I don't want to be greedy. But that twerp Lionel is another matter. He'll definitely have to go—but with Lily Quench and her dragon out there, there's no guarantee that's going to happen."

"I've never even seen this famous dragon," said General Sark coldly. "For all I know, it doesn't exist outside your little purple head."

"You'll know it when a thousand-ton, fire-breathing lizard comes flying over your battlements, cutie," said Crystal. "For the last time, Sark. Lily Quench is here in the citadel. The dragon can't be far behind. Just don't say I didn't warn you."

"You have warned me. Over and over again, like a stuck record." General Sark picked up his hat and pulled on his greatcoat. "Why don't you just buzz off, Crystal? Stop hassling me, and I might be nice and not send you to the worst mine in the Black Mountains." He put on his hat and stormed out of the room.

"You'll be sorry you said that," said Crystal to the door as it closed behind him. If Evangeline had been there, she would have known at once there was trouble brewing. But Evangeline had troubles of her own to deal with. With a flick of her purple curls, Crystal hopped down from Gordon's desk and purposefully left the room.

Huddled in her blue coat, Angela climbed softly up the stairs that led to the pigeon loft. Above her she could hear the pigeons cooing softly. A draft of cold air came down the staircase, and the metal steps were dotted white with bird droppings. In her hand she carried a strip of paper, folded very small and squeezed into a tiny metal capsule.

Angela thought anxiously of Gordon. She did not know where he was or even if he was still alive. But with the exception of one other person, Angela loved Gordon more than anyone else in the world. For this reason she was as sure as she ever could be that she was doing the right thing.

Angela entered the loft and ran her eyes along the line of cages. When she found the one marked **CAMP I: SQUAD I,** she picked out the biggest, strongest-looking bird, tied her message capsule hastily to its leg, and tossed it out of the window. For a split second it fell. Then it recovered and, with a flurry of wings, started flapping off on its way to the Ashby border.

"Now what do we do?" said Gordon, when he'd finished yelling at no one in particular. He hadn't really expected anyone to listen, but he was so used to getting what he wanted, it had seemed the natural thing to do.

"I think there's a flashlight in my backpack," said Lily. "You were holding it when they locked the door. It's in the side pocket."

"Hang on." There was a moment's pause while Gordon unzipped the pack. Something fell on the floor with a clatter. "Got it," said Gordon, and the flashlight flicked on.

"Well, at least that's better." Lily held out her hand for her backpack, and, rather to his surprise, Gordon gave it to her. Lily knelt and started rummaging through her things.

"I don't suppose you've got any food in there?" asked Gordon. It had been several hours since lunch, and it had just occurred to him that it might be a long time before he got anything else to eat.

"I told you—the bear got it." Lily found what she was looking for at the bottom of the bag. "Have you any idea what's happening?"

"Not really," Gordon admitted. "But there was something fishy happening earlier this afternoon. You see, General Sark was drilling the troops. And then he made me go out on that patrol."

"Who's General Sark?" Lily asked, and Gordon told her. He told her a lot more, too, about his father and the Ashby Invasion, about how Sark didn't like him, and how someone had tried to kill him on the obstacle course. Lily let him talk, and all the while she worked at the lock on the door with her skeleton key. Jason had taught her how to pick locks with it before she left, saying it was sure to come in handy someday. At the time Lily hadn't entirely believed him, but she was very glad now he'd done it.

At last the lock clicked open. Lily opened the door and went out into the dimly lit passageway. A woman in a long brown fur, with a smart round hat on her head, was walking in their direction. She looked vaguely familiar, and Lily blinked.

Then a voice drawled, "Lily Quench, or I'm an elephant."

Lily gasped. It was Queen Evangeline's mother, Crystal Bright.

chapter ten

Escape to the Mountains

"Crystal! What are you doing here?" burst out Lily.

Crystal bridled. "Your Majesty, thank you! Or at the very least, Mrs. Bright to a twerp like you. As to what I'm doing here, miss, I could say the same to you."

"I'm on an official Quenching Expedition for King Lionel," said Lily. "Nobody told me *you'd* be here."

"That's because *my* mission is top secret," said Crystal. "My daughter, Queen Evangeline, sent me here as—as ambassador to the Black Empire."

"Ambassador? I don't believe a w—"

"I haven't got time for this," Gordon interrupted. "Something's been happening in the citadel. I've got to find out what."

"As to that," said Crystal, with a toss of her purple curls, "if you really want to know, I can tell you. That creep, Sark, has taken over. He's planning to throw out the count and make himself ruler of the Black Empire."

Gordon went white with shock. "Throw out my father? I've got to do something!"

"Too late!" said Crystal cheerfully. "If I were you, cutie, I'd hoof it out of here *pronto*. Sark's already got patrols out looking for you. You're next on his hit list."

"How do you know all this?" said Lily suspiciously. Despite what Crystal had said, Lily knew far too much about her not to be worried about what she was doing. But before she could ask Crystal any more awkward questions, the sound of footsteps stopped their conversation dead. A Black Squad had turned the corner of the concrete passage and was marching loudly toward them.

"Run!" shouted Lily. Gordon reached out a

hand and slapped a red switch on the passage wall. An alarm rang, and a huge metal door swung shut across the passage between them and the soldiers. Crystal ran over and frantically banged her fists against the metal door. On the other side they could hear shouts and then the sounds of boots kicking the steel.

"Let me out! Let me out!" Crystal shouted.

Lily grabbed her wrist.

"Let me go!"

"No way! You're coming with us!" Months of digging gardens on Skansey had made Lily strong. She dug her fingernails into Crystal's wrist and yanked her determinedly into a run.

"Ow! Ow, you little brute! I'll tell Lionel on you! I'll tell the queen! All right, all right, I'm coming!" A great rending crash sounded behind them as the metal door was smashed down. Soldiers started pouring through the gap, and Crystal jumped and squawked like a chicken on its way to the chopping block. At the end of the passage, Lily skidded around a corner and came up against a blank wall.

"Not that way!" Gordon paused momentarily to shut another gate, flung open a door, and pushed them through. They turned a corner and pelted down some stairs to a lower level. At the bottom they bumped into a guard, standing sentry at the entrance to a cell. Lily and Crystal screamed, but Gordon merely yelled at him, "Out of my way, idiot!" and the man fell back against the wall without another word.

At the end of the passage was another door. Gordon fumbled inside his pocket, and Lily, a few paces behind him, paused to glance through a window into an adjacent room. Inside she saw a garage filled with motorcycles, armored cars—and soldiers. One looked up. Lily ducked, but it was too late.

"They've seen us!" she shouted, and ran the last few steps to the end of the passage. Gordon was already forcing a key into a lock. A voice shouted for them to halt. Lily threw herself into darkness, and then Gordon slammed the door and locked it.

He snapped on a light. Lily saw a sleek, beautiful black-and-chrome motorcycle and sidecar. She wrenched open the door of the sidecar and crammed Crystal inside. Gordon jumped onto the bike and pulled on his helmet.

Lily grabbed the second one from the shelf and scrambled onto the seat.

Gordon fired up the bike and hit the button for the automatic door. He revved up the engine and flicked on the headlight. Exhaust fumes filled the garage as the door started slowly going up. Behind them there was a loud banging and clattering of boots against the steel. "Come on, come on!" Gordon muttered with a backward glance, and then the door was up, he hit the accelerator, and they shot out of the garage into the night.

Out on the mountainside it was dark, starless, and bitterly cold. Lily was still wearing her flying jacket and hat, but she had forgotten to put on her gloves, and her hands quickly became numb. She couldn't begin to imagine what Gordon felt like. He had taken his greatcoat off in the citadel and was wearing nothing but his uniform and helmet.

The road was black and icy, uphill all the way. The great bike purred effortlessly around the bends, its headlight sweeping over boulders, snow, and yellow ice. They crossed a river, running in a torrent over jagged rocks, and roared through a cluster of dismal-looking buildings. On the next bend, Lily happened to glance back. A beam of light swept across the visor of her helmet, and she froze in horror.

"They're chasing us!" Lily tapped Gordon's helmet. He turned his head, dropped down a gear, and accelerated until it was all Lily could do to hold on. Behind them, a trail of headlights dodged and fluttered across the road. Lily realized that, fast as they were traveling, it was not going to be fast enough. Without the added weight of the sidecar and two extra passengers, it would be no time at all before their pursuers caught up and forced them off the road.

As if he could read Lily's thoughts, Gordon revved the bike until it screamed. A huge tunnel yawned in front of them, low and wide, and he shot inside. At once the crosswinds stopped buffeting them. Electric light glared harshly down, and the high whine of the bike's engine echoed off the smooth concrete walls. Lily looked back over her shoulder again. Ten or twelve black motorbikes, with Black Squad soldiers in the saddles, were just entering the tunnel behind them. One bike was ahead of the rest and gaining rapidly.

If we go any faster we'll crash, thought Lily. She glanced back again and saw the rider of the leading bike lift his hand and point a remote control at a spot on the wall ahead. A heavy-duty motor ground into life and a huge metal door started dropping down across the road at the exit end of the tunnel.

"Duck!" Despite her helmet, Lily heard Gordon's scream. She ducked, the bike flew under the closing door, and she almost felt her helmet graze the metal. Then they were through, and the door clanged shut. There was a tremendous crash as their pursuer hit the metal at full speed, and they were away into the night with only the sound of their own engine in their ears.

In her cave on the top of Dragon's Neck, Queen Dragon lay sleeping. She dreamed she was flying through the air with the clouds tickling her scales, and a companion was with her—not Lily or any of her human friends, but another dragon whom she had not seen for hundreds of years. Together they soared over snow-covered peaks that were higher even than the Black Mountains, headed for a country of dragons that had been lost for centuries, and was remembered only in dreams.

As she and her companion flew over the final peak into a valley so green and beautiful no human could bear the sight of it, a flight of other dragons came winging toward them, their scales winking green, red, and bronze in the summer sunshine. Queen Dragon gave a snort of delight that sent a fireball shooting through the clear air like a firework. She and her companion drew in their wings and dived down through the balmy air to meet their friends—

"Queen Dragon!"

A familiar voice broke through her slumber, sending the beautiful dream spinning away in a thousand pieces. Queen Dragon groaned and opened her eyes. It was bitterly cold, and she was still in that wretched cave on Dragon's Neck, waiting for Lily and Mr. Hartley to return. But it was not Lily's voice that had woken her up. Queen Dragon blinked, turned her massive head, and jumped with fright. Standing a short distance away from her were two small figures dressed in Black Squad uniforms.

"It's all right, Queen Dragon, it's only me!" said the taller figure hastily as Queen Dragon half lunged toward it. "It's Lionel—and this is Evangeline. We're in disguise."

"But what are you doing here?" asked Queen Dragon after the first shock had passed. "How did you get here? And how did you find me?"

"It was my idea," said Evangeline modestly. "We drove up to the Black Mountains in Zouche's old armored car, and when we ran out of road we got out and started climbing toward the smoke puffs. I don't know whether you realize you smoke when you sleep. As to what we're doing here, we've come to warn you and Lily." She looked around the cave. "Where *is* Lily?"

"With Mr. Hartley, of course," Queen Dragon said. "They've gone to look for the blue lily in Dragon's Downfall."

"Oh, dear," said Lionel. "Then we're too late."

"Too late? What do you mean?" Queen

Dragon started anxiously puffing smoke. "What's happening? What's gone wrong?"

"It's a long story, Queen Dragon," said Evangeline. "Sit down and we'll tell you everything, right from the beginning."

Speeding along the mountain road below the peak where Queen Dragon was hiding, Lily was startled by a series of alarming sounds from the bike. It backfired, put-puttered, and then backfired again. Gordon revved desperately, but the dying engine went finally, abruptly, dead. The bike coasted along for a short distance, slowed, and stopped.

"What's happened?" Lily jumped down and pulled off her helmet. Crystal flung open the sidecar door and scrambled out onto the road. Gordon threw his helmet into the snow and kicked the exhaust pipe in a fit of temper. But there was nothing he could do. The bike was out of gas.

"Now what?" asked Lily. Gordon shrugged. All he had been worried about was escaping. He'd never given a moment's thought to whether the bike had fuel.

"I'm cold," Crystal complained. She stamped her feet and shivered.

"If that's your teeth chattering, they're awfully loud," remarked Lily. Gordon looked up from the bike.

"That's not her teeth." He stood listening for a moment, and the sound resolved into a low ominous buzz that grew louder and louder. Suddenly yellow searchlights broke the darkness. Traveling in tight formation, a sinister column of flying black shapes appeared over the crest of the mountain.

"Dragonets!" shouted Gordon. "They're fighting dragonets, and they're deadly!"

chapter eleven

Attack of the Dragonets

Crystal looked up in amazement. "Dragons! Baby dragons!"

"They're not dragons," snarled Gordon. "I told you: they're dragonets—flying fighting machines. Quick! Over there, behind those rocks! Hurry!"

They darted off the road and started scrambling through the snow to some rocks at the foot of a nearby cliff. Lily fell into a drift and disappeared almost up to her waist. Gordon stopped to pull her out. The tiny dragons flew closer and closer. One broke free from formation and swooped low overhead. A strange smell filled the air, like a car exhaust, and a streak of fire streamed from its wing. There was a bang and a spatter of melted snow from the overhanging cliff. Gordon gave Lily one last, enormous tug, and she fell forward out of the snowdrift. She scrambled to her feet and together they ran and dived behind the rocks.

A bomb exploded behind them, and showers of snow flew up, leaving a blackened crater. The explosion was followed by another, then another. A flying sliver of ice cut Gordon on the cheek, and Lily, crouched on the end, was knocked flat by a deluge of snow. Then, just as they thought the bombardment would never stop, the last dragonet dropped its bomb. It swooped low overhead—so low that Lily could see a pilot sitting behind the mechanical creature's glowing eyes—then buzzed away to rejoin its companions.

"Their bombs can't hit us here under the cliff," she said. "And they're too heavy to land on the snow."

"The dragonets weren't designed to fight here," said Gordon. "They were built for the invasion of Ashby. Look out! They're coming back."

The dragonets had regrouped a short distance

away and were heading toward them like a swarm of evil bees. This time the bombs started exploding high above their heads. On the third explosion, half a dozen small rocks came rattling down, followed by a boulder the size of an armchair. Then, with a great rumbling, roaring crash, a huge chunk of cliff fell right in front of them. It bounced twice, spraying snow and gravel everywhere, then slewed around and came to a stop just in front of them. Everyone screamed and ducked, cowering for cover.

"They're going to kill us!" Crystal wailed. Smaller rocks were still falling, every one of them big enough to brain any person silly or unlucky enough to get in its way. Lily clutched the rocky outcrop, feeling faint and breathless.

"No," said Gordon suddenly. "You're wrong. Look. That big bit of cliff has given us some real shelter. Unless they bring the whole cliff down on top of us, for a little while we're safe."

"They're not going to give up, though, surely?" said Lily.

Gordon shook his head. "Oh, no. General Sark is after me. He doesn't dare risk my escaping and reaching my father."

Lily began to recover a little. "We can't wait here," she said. "We'll freeze."

"We'll be dead long before that," said Gordon. "Sark will send in his ground troops next. They'll have skis and snowmobiles. They're used to moving around in this sort of weather. I'd say we've got half an hour at the most."

Another bomb fell overhead, and another. Then Lily heard the dragonets flying away again, their eerie buzz fading to silence in the clear mountain air. Beneath her flying jacket, she could feel the scales tingling on her elbow.

"We need Queen Dragon here," she said slowly. "Those dragonet things were metal, and they weren't very big. Queen Dragon could have eaten them in a single gulp, the way she did with Miss Moldavia's sports car. I think our only hope is to try and meet up with her."

"We've lost the bike," Crystal pointed out.

"I'm not talking about the bike," said Lily. "Listen. Last winter, when we were living together on the Island of Skansey, Queen Dragon taught me the Dragons' Cry of Summoning. It's a magical call that a dragon makes when its life is in the deadliest danger. If Queen Dragon hears it, she should come at once to help us."

Crystal was outraged. "You mean you could have got us out of this before now?"

"If there's no other dragon within hearing, the call rebounds on the dragon who made it," explained Lily. "It's so powerful, it could kill me."

"Well, if you don't make the call, the dragonets will kill you anyway," said Crystal. "So what's stopping you?"

"Nothing," said Lily with dignity, and she scrambled up on top of the rock and closed her eyes.

Lily stood feeling the cold wind on her face, the gentle icy touch of the snowflakes, until she grew calm. She started thinking herself into being a dragon. She felt the scales tingling on her arm and imagined them spreading all over her body. Then she felt the dragon's fire inside her and was no longer cold. Deep within, the sound of the Dragons' Cry of Summoning formed into a stream of something like smoke and fire. It coiled around her insides and surged up until Lily could no longer hold it in. She opened her mouth, and the cry rang out across the frosty mountains, from peak to peak, valley to valley, a harsh, beautiful note no human throat ought to have been able to make, a sound that belonged to the world of the dragons that had perished long ago.

The cry faded out. For a moment there was silence. And then, as Lily's cold, terrified companions watched and waited for something to happen, the answer came back on a lower note, a call of love and support that could only have come from a dragon's throat.

Lily opened her eyes. She stood quite still, staring blankly at the others. Then a snowflake fell softly on her cheek, and she brushed it away.

"It's all right," she said. "She's heard us. She's coming right away."

Long before the first snowmobiles arrived at the foot of the cliff, the fugitives had gone, leaving nothing behind but some footprints and a large patch of melted snow where Queen Dragon had landed. Even Gordon's bike had disappeared. Queen Dragon, who had been feeling hungry after her long sleep in the cave, had politely asked its owner if she could eat it. Gordon had been so overwhelmed by the sight of her, he had not known how to say no.

"Mother, how could you?" fumed Evangeline when they were all reunited in the cave. "Somebody ought to lock you up, the things you do."

Crystal sniffed. "Just you try it, miss."

"One day I might. For your own good," said Evangeline. "You could have been killed."

"Yes. I suppose I could," said Crystal thoughtfully, and then suddenly the reality of what had happened hit her, and she sat down with a thump and burst into tears.

In a sheltered corner of the cave, Lionel was laying out a picnic supper on a blanket. In another corner, Gordon sat with his head in his arms. In the cavern mouth, Lily and Queen Dragon were cooking sausages. Queen Dragon was having to supply the fire for the cooking, something that was easier said than done in a small space.

"Ouch! Turn it down, turn it down!" yelped Lily, dropping the pan with a clang onto the cavern floor. A few scorched bits of bread fell to the ground, and she scooped them up. But at last everything was cooked and the travelers sat down to a picnic supper. Because of the unexpected guests, there was not quite enough to go around, but Lily was so hungry she was grateful for every mouthful. Gordon, however, ate hardly anything. Halfway through the meal, he stood up abruptly and went to sit at the cave entrance by himself.

"I suppose we should go back to Ashby now," said Lionel when they had eaten everything. "Lily, I don't suppose you finished your quest?"

"The blue lily's in my pocket," said Lily. "But we can't go back to Ashby yet, Your Majesty. Mr. Hartley is still a prisoner in the citadel."

There was an uncomfortable silence.

"Lily," said Evangeline gently, "I'm so sorry to have to tell you this, but... it seems Mr. Hartley wasn't the friend we thought he was. That's why we came here, to warn you. Mr. Hartley has been coming to the Black Mountains for years. He's a spy."

Lily looked from Evangeline to Lionel. Their expressions were so grave she knew they were deadly serious.

"There must be a mistake," Lily said. "Mr. Hartley wouldn't do that."

"No, Lily," said Lionel. "There's no mistake. We found the notes in his diary back in Ashby."

"But Mr. Hartley told me he'd been to the Black Mountains looking for someone," said Lily. She remembered something else. "He told me about it in Dragon's Downfall, when he saved my life. He said he thought of a special person who was lost to him. Remembering her gave him the strength to fight the magic."

Evangeline looked doubtful. "I've never heard Mr. Hartley mention anybody special."

"That doesn't mean she doesn't exist." Lily sat forward. "Don't you see! It must be the reason he's been coming here!" She turned to Lionel. "It must be true. It must!"

"It might be," said Lionel. "But, Lily, even if it is true, there's nothing we can do about it. Mr. Hartley is inside the Black Citadel. There's no way we can rescue him."

"There is! I know there is! I'll go myself!"

"No."

"Mr. Hartley would have done it for me!"

"Lily, I said no." Lionel spoke in his sternest, most kingly-sounding voice. "It's far too dangerous. I am the king of Ashby, and you are my official Quencher, and I am *commanding* you to obey me."

Everyone looked shocked, even Queen Dragon. It was the first time Lionel had ever commanded Lily to do anything. Then Crystal suddenly shrieked and jumped to her feet.

"My fur! My mink, it's missing! Where's that Gordon? The little brute has stolen my mink coat!"

"It's all right, Crystal. Calm down," said Lionel. "Gordon was just sitting in the entrance. He probably borrowed it because he was cold."

"I wouldn't be so sure about that." Evangeline went over to the mouth of the cave and peered out into the swiftly falling snow. "I can't see him anywhere, and there are footsteps going down the hill. It looks to me like he's run away."

chapter twelve
Dragon's Downfall

Gordon had vanished. Nobody knew where he had gone, but for Lily it was easy to guess. Since he couldn't go back to the citadel, he had to press onward, along the eastern flank of Dragon's Neck and down into Dragon's Downfall. Lily couldn't begin to imagine what he was planning to do there. Perhaps he hadn't been thinking clearly when he left. Their only hope now was to find him before he went too far.

Gordon had no food and no warm clothes except Crystal's coat. His only piece of equipment was Lily's flashlight, which he had put in his pocket back in the citadel. Nobody could work out why he had done it. Except, perhaps, Lionel.

"Gordon is the Black Count's son," he said. "He knows how valuable he is as a hostage. Come on, Evie. Can you honestly tell me you haven't thought of taking him back to Ashby and using him to force the count to stop invading us?"

Evangeline blushed as red as Queen Dragon's scales. "We would never have hurt him," she said defensively.

"We know that. But Gordon doesn't. He's afraid, and he doesn't trust us. He only joined forces with Lily because of circumstances. Someone will have to go and look for him."

"He can't have got very far on foot," said Lily. "Queen Dragon and I will go."

Queen Dragon looked glum. "I was afraid you'd say that," she said.

"Don't be silly, Queen Dragon." Lily was already packing her equipment into a sack. "I'll come with you. You'll be perfectly safe."

"Famous last words," said Queen Dragon, but for once, she made no further protest. A few moments later she and Lily took off. They circled once over Dragon's Neck, then vanished into the night.

Gordon was exhausted. He'd had a long and terrifying day and was hungry and frozen stiff. Several times during his journey in the dark he'd wanted to stop and rest, but he'd heard too many horror stories of people falling asleep and dying in the snow to let himself do that. Mostly, though, he kept on moving because he wanted to put as much distance as possible between himself and the cave on Dragon's Neck. Gordon was afraid. Afraid of General Sark who had done the unthinkable and turned against his father. And afraid, too, of Lily Quench and her friends: the cold-eyed Crystal, and Lionel and Evangeline, who claimed to be king and queen of Ashby, that strange little country where all this trouble had started.

By the time he'd left the cave, Gordon had half convinced himself that Lionel and Evangeline were working with General Sark. In his heart, he knew this was wrong. Sark had obviously been planning his takeover for ages. But Lionel was so honest looking, Gordon was sure he must be superdevious underneath, while Evangeline had a disconcerting way of looking at people, as if she was somehow seeing right inside them. As for Queen Dragon... Gordon shivered as he remembered the way she'd casually chomped up his motorbike. Queen Dragon was terrifying. At all costs, he had to find his father and warn him just how dangerous she was.

By the time the sun came up, the battery in Lily's flashlight was almost dead. Gordon had covered a lot of ground, but he was also lost. He sat down in the shelter of a rock and ate some snow and a sticky toffee out of one of Crystal's pockets. It was a poor sort of breakfast, but it made him feel a bit better, and the pale winter sunshine cheered him up. After a short rest he headed off again. Gordon wasn't really sure where he was, but he figured it must be one of the valleys to the north of Dragon's Neck, and that sooner or later he would come across someone who would help.

Five minutes later he saw a strange-looking stone ahead of him. It was very tall and had a hole in the middle of it. For the first time since leaving the cave, Gordon started to have an inkling that his wanderings in the dark might have taken him somewhere he hadn't intended. Gordon remembered what Lily Quench had said about picking flowers in Dragon's Downfall and how he'd thought she'd been lying. Now he desperately found himself hoping she had been telling the truth.

Lily and Queen Dragon had been searching for Gordon for hours. Back and forth, to and fro, Queen Dragon flew over snowfields and slopes, while Lily scanned the landscape with her night goggles. But there were no telltale movements against the whiteness, no dark shadows or tracks in the snow, nothing to prove that Gordon had even passed through. When dawn broke, with no sign of him anywhere, the rescuers were cold, tired, and starting to despair.

"Let's have a rest," said Queen Dragon, and she swooped down and landed on a ridge of rock. Lily scrambled down, feeling stiff and sore.

"I hope Gordon's all right," she said. "Suppose he's fallen into a crevasse?"

"If he has, we'll never find him," said Queen Dragon. "But if you ask me, that little creep knew exactly what he was doing. It wouldn't surprise me to discover that he's got friends who are helping him. The best thing for us to do is leave this nasty place and go home."

"Go home? No way!" said Lily. "Queen Dragon, what a coward you are! Look at you! A dragon the size of a house, and you're behaving like a gutless wimp."

Queen Dragon drew herself up. Her yellow eyes rolled alarmingly. "Don't say that, Lily. It isn't kind."

"It's true, though." Lily was tired and fed up. For the first time since leaving Ashby, she lost her temper. "Ever since King Lionel suggested this mission, you've been carrying on like a baby. Saying you can't go, trembling and shaking from head to foot. Only you've never told me exactly what it is you're frightened of. Well, I'm sick of it, Queen Dragon. I'm starting to think it's all an excuse."

"It's not an excuse," said Queen Dragon,

looking hurt. "It's real. I just can't tell you. It's a secret. A dragon secret. That's why I can't tell you, Lily. What happened here is a secret only dragons can know."

"A secret only dragons can know?" Lily slipped her arm out of her jacket and rolled back her sleeve. "Then what about this? Look at these scales on my elbow. They're dragon scales, just like yours. Quenches and dragons might have been enemies for hundreds of years, but we're friends now, and always will be. And friends don't have secrets from one another."

Queen Dragon stared at the shiny, scaly patch on Lily's arm. It glistened in the moonlight, pale and flesh-colored, but dragonish all the same. It looked, thought Lily, like the soft new flesh on the tummy of a baby dragon, and then she wondered where that thought had come from. She had never seen a baby dragon. But she knew she was right. Between Quenches and dragons, there was hardly any difference. That was why, for so many centuries, Quenches had been the best dragon slayers around.

A dragon tear fell—*splash!*—on the rock in front of her, like a bucket of boiling water. But

Lily did not duck or run away. Instead she climbed back up onto Queen Dragon's mighty snout and sat down on its hot rough scales. All at once, everything around her went deathly still. The pupils of Queen Dragon's eyes grew wide until they were filled with a darkness so deep Lily felt she was drowning in it.

A picture appeared in Queen Dragon's eyes. At first it looked like an old film with faraway jerky images, and then it grew clear and focused. Lily realized she was looking back at the Black Mountains as they had been thousands of years ago. The skies teemed with fighting dragons. They smashed into one another in midair, tore at one another's flesh with their wicked teeth, blasted one another with fires so hot they turned into charred skeletons that fell from the sky and shattered on the rocks. Blood rained over the cliffs of Dragon's Downfall, and the boiling river below was filled with dead and dying dragons. In the Great War of the Dragons only the very oldest and youngest who could not fight had survived.

The picture slowly faded from Queen Dragon's eyes. "I told you this is a bad place, Lily," she said in a small, sad voice. "Now you know why. The

Great War of the Dragons happened when I was scarcely out of the egg. Since then, not one dragon who's gone to Dragon's Downfall has come back from it alive."

Lily laid a comforting hand on Queen Dragon's head. "No, Queen Dragon," she said. "You're wrong. I came back. And if I can go into Dragon's Downfall and survive, then so can you."

Standing beside the stone with the hole in it, Gordon heard the buzz of dragonets overhead and knew he had been discovered.

He looked up. A dark row of dots was advancing toward him across the wintry sky, and in all the vast expanse of white that surrounded him, there was nowhere to hide. Gordon remembered how excited he'd been when he'd visited the dragonet factory with his father. Now a sick fear filled the pit of his stomach. Gordon's hands sweated in his pockets and he half smelled, half tasted the bitterly cold mountain air as if nothing had ever been so fresh, so precious, so good.

The dragonets headed toward him like malevolent insects. They would be able to see him by now, a small dark target against the snow. Then, to his astonishment, Gordon saw that another, larger dragonet had silently appeared behind the rest. It was flying much faster than the others, and it was not black, but red. A tiny human figure was sitting on its head, and as Gordon excitedly recognized Lily and Queen Dragon, a great gush of flame and fire came streaming from the dragon's mouth.

With a hideous mechanical screaming sound, the charred remains of the last three dragonets fell out of the sky and hit the ground, sending ice and melted snow flying up like a fountain. Shocked into action, the rest of the formation broke up, but Queen Dragon was too big and fast and agile. Like a frog catching flies from a lily pad, she gulped the next three dragonets down in quick succession, and when the last one turned and started firing at her, she merely blinked. Queen Dragon's mighty crimson tail flicked up casually, just once, as if she was swatting a mosquito. The last of the attackers lost control and exploded in midair.

Gordon cheered with excitement. Then he belatedly remembered that Queen Dragon and her friends were as much his enemies as General Sark. He turned and started running away across the snowfield in the direction of a nearby cliff.

"Gordon! Gordon, stop!" cried a familiar voice, but Gordon didn't stop. Another voice was calling him from the edge of the cliff—a small voice like a young child's, very clear and sweet. Footsteps pounded in the snow behind him, and the voice urged him on, telling him to hurry, that they were about to catch him. The edge of the cliff was just before him when a flying tackle brought him down. Gordon lashed out with his fists and boots, but his pursuer was sitting beside him, grabbing his wrists with a grip like iron and wrenching him back from the edge. A loud voice called his name, and the mist parted below him. He saw the dizzying depths and the jagged rocks waiting below him and looked up into the face of his rescuer.

It was his father.

chapter thirteen

The Black Count

"Hello, Father," said Gordon stupidly. He turned his head and realized just how close he was lying to the edge of the cliff. Below him something small and golden stood on a rocky ledge. It looked like a statue, but the wind was blowing water mist up from the rapids below and blocked his view.

The count stood up, his dark general's cape billowing in the wind. Released from his grip, Gordon rolled away from the edge and scrambled to his feet.

"How did you get here?" he asked.

"By dragonet," said the count. "Angela sent a message, telling me what Sark had done. She waited for me outside the citadel, and when I arrived we followed the other dragonets to this valley."

"General Sark." Gordon looked alarmed. "Father, the rebellion—"

Gordon's father cut him off. "It's of no consequence, Gordon. Our family has ruled the Black Empire for centuries. Never forget that. It will take more than someone like Sark to change things." He looked around. "So this is Dragon's Downfall. It's hard to see what people are so frightened of."

"It's an evil place," said Gordon with a shiver. "Didn't you hear that thing over the cliff, calling you to jump?"

"Of course not," said the count. "It's only a statue. And there is no such thing as evil, Gordon. It's only your fear that makes you say that."

Gordon said nothing. He wanted to believe what his father said, but after the events of the last few weeks he found he could not. For there *was* such a thing as evil. It had made Jacobsen and Harries try to kill him on the obstacle course, and had caused Sark to usurp his father's empire. And countless years ago a great evil had fashioned the golden statue under the cliff, an evil that drew on people's weaknesses and lured them to their deaths. Only people who were full of love could resist it. Only people as wicked as the magic were oblivious to it. Which meant... Troubled and confused, Gordon turned to his father, an unspoken question on his lips. But the count was looking away from him. Uphill, Queen Dragon and Lily had landed on the snow and were standing talking with a woman in a familiar blue coat.

"Angela!"

Angela heard Gordon's voice and looked up. She started to walk down the hill toward him, and, at the sight of her, Gordon felt a surge of relief and love. He wanted to run up and give her an enormous hug. If his father hadn't been watching, he probably would have.

Angela came over to where Gordon and his father were standing. Her smile told Gordon that she was thinking of him and how glad she felt he was safe. She put her arm around his shoulders and lovingly ruffled his hair. Then she went and looked curiously over the edge of the cliff at the statue on the ledge below. A shiver went down Gordon's spine again. This time he knew for certain what it meant.

"What do we do now?" he asked, feeling he had to say something.

Angela looked at the count. But before either of them had a chance to answer Gordon's question, they were interrupted by the purring sound of an approaching snowmobile. Gordon saw it crest the hill behind them. Lily ran to Queen Dragon, and Queen Dragon's wings flapped in panic.

The snowmobile, a sleek black new one, came skimming down the hill and stopped close by them. It looked like the one Gordon's father used, only the crest had been painted out and a new one stuck on top. As Gordon watched, the front door opened and a handcuffed prisoner was dropped headfirst out into the snow. Lily screamed, Angela went white, and Queen Dragon uttered a high-pitched squawk of alarm.

"Mr. Hartley!"

"Stand still." Four Black Squad soldiers jumped out of the snowmobile and raised their weapons.

Then the back door opened and out climbed General Sark.

"Well, well," he said unpleasantly. "So here you are. You've caused me a lot of trouble, young Gordon. I've been looking for you everywhere. And to find your father here, too! I never thought I'd be so lucky.

"If you or Miss Quench come any closer, lizard," Sark called to Queen Dragon, "your friend Hartley here will be dropped off the cliff. Understood?"

Lily nodded, and Queen Dragon stopped flapping and grew quiet. Gordon looked at the bound prisoner lying in the snow and recognized the man he had captured with Lily at the campsite in the gully. The man's glasses were broken and dangling awkwardly off one ear, and his face was covered with bruises, but, oddly enough, he was smiling. It was then that Gordon realized with a shock he was looking at Angela. Angela, in turn, was looking wonderingly back at him.

"You're alive!" she said softly. "They told me you were dead, but I always hoped you'd find me."

"They told me you were dead, too," said Mr. Hartley, and his voice was strong and full of love. "But I never stopped looking and praying that I'd find you. Now I'm going to take you home to Ashby."

"Ashby!" The expression on Angela's face as she said the word made Gordon feel like he was going to die. It was as if someone had stuck a knife into him and was wiggling it around in his heart. He had always thought Angela loved him. Now she was leaving. Without so much as a backward glance she was going back to that horrible little tinpot country, and he would never see her again.

"No!" he burst out. "You can't do this. You can't leave me! You promised!"

Angela jerked up her head. "Gordon, what do you mean? This is my *husband*."

"I don't care!" Gordon yelled. "You can't have a husband. Not unless I say so. You're not allowed to love anyone but me!"

"Gordon, I *do* love you—" Angela began, but Gordon could listen to her no longer. A horrible rage billowed up inside him, white and hot. With a cry of fury, he threw himself forward and cannoned into her where she was standing on the edge of the cliff.

Angela went sprawling. Lily screamed, Mr. Hartley yelled, and Angela gave a piercing cry as she skidded over the edge. Only the count kept his head. Somehow, in the melee of bodies on the cliff top, he grabbed the collar of Angela's blue coat and kept tight hold of it.

What happened next, Gordon could never exactly say. One moment, Angela was dangling over the cliff grabbing frantically for a spur of rock; the next, she was clinging to it with one hand, and the count was trying to haul her up. Gordon heard a rumble in the ice beneath him and threw himself backward. Angela grabbed the rocky spur with her other hand and started clawing her way to safety, but the count was still standing alone on a narrow precipice of nothing more than ice and compacted snow.

"Father! Watch out!" Gordon shouted. The count turned and tensed to spring. As he did, Gordon looked into his face. He saw no fear, no anger, no despair there, but an expression flickered in the count's eyes. In that moment something dreadful, dark, and precious passed between them.

Words formed on Gordon's lips, but he did not say them. Then, before the count could make the leap to safety, the icy precipice gave way under his weight. There was a roar of breaking ice and snow as he vanished, and the sound was lost forever in the deafening roar of the river below. "No!" screamed Gordon. *"No!"*

He whirled around, broke through the confused ranks of the Black Squad soldiers, and started running away up the hill. General Sark snapped an order, and two soldiers broke ranks and pelted after him. But it was too late for anyone to stop him. Just as his pursuers caught up with him, Gordon reached the stone with the hole in it. He dived forward. One of the soldiers grabbed his ankle, but he kicked out and his boot came off in the man's hand. In a second Gordon had wriggled through the hole—and vanished into thin air.

"Follow him!" roared Sark. "Follow him!" But the soldiers were not so silly as that. They stood for a moment, looking at the hole in the rock, and then one of them put his hand in and jerked it back as if he had been stung.

Mr. Hartley staggered to his feet. "I wouldn't

make them go through it if I were you," he said. "There's no guarantee they'll end up in the same place as Gordon, and it's highly unlikely they'll be able to come back. You might understand the magic that governs that stone. I only know it's a bad thing which was erected for a bad purpose."

"Like the Golden Child," said Lily, venturing forward. "Have you seen it, General?"

Sark looked at her distrustfully. "The golden what?"

"Oh, it's nothing, really," said Lily. "Just a statue made out of solid gold, down the cliff there."

Sark took a step toward the cliff. Lily caught her breath. But at the last moment the general changed his mind. He threw back his head and laughed.

"Hah! A golden statue? Up here, in the middle of nowhere? Do you think I'm silly enough to believe that?"

"Perhaps not," said Mr. Hartley. "However, I do know only somebody truly stupid would leave a snowmobile parked where a hungry dragon could find it." A loud crunching sounded behind them. As Sark and his soldiers took one look at Queen Dragon chomping into their snowmobile and started running for their lives, Mr. Hartley added, "And don't go asking us for any lifts home, either."

"Be careful, Queen Dragon," Lily warned her. "You're getting awfully close to the edge there. You must keep out of range of the Golden Child."

"I'm all right, Lily," Queen Dragon assured her. "I was just hungry, that's all. You know, this place doesn't seem as bad as I expected. If we could only get rid of that statue—"

"Maybe we *can* get rid of it," said Lily. "All sorts of things can happen now. Just wait until I tell Lionel the Black Count is gone!"

But Angela shook her head. "No, Lily," she said somberly. "You're wrong. The Black Count hasn't gone. His name is Gordon, and he went through the hole in the stone not ten minutes ago."

chapter fourteen

King Dragon

When a dragon dies, its bones slowly petrify, and its scales become flakes of glass. The river that ran through Dragon's Downfall was the graveyard of all who were killed in the Great War of the Dragons. The Golden Child had lured them in, and their greed and fear and anger had turned them against one another. Now their glassy scales were scattered over the jagged cliffs, and their bones were the rocks that formed the rapids in the river below.

Lily pulled down the hood on the fireproof cloak that had belonged to her dragon-slaying ancestor, Mad Brian Quench. She climbed up onto Queen Dragon's head. "You can do it, Queen Dragon," she whispered. "I know you can."

"I hope so."

While Mr. Hartley and Angela watched from a safe distance, Queen Dragon and Lily took flight and circled out over the river. Everything below was ice and snow and sharp black rock. From the air Lily could make out the rocky skeletons of dead dragons, lying in sinuous lines along the floor of the gorge. There were so many she could not have hoped to count them, and she turned her eyes resolutely to the cliff ahead. Halfway up, the Golden Child was winking in the sunlight. It was hard to imagine how it had ever been put in its place, if not by some magic as strong and evil as the thing itself.

Closer...closer...Any moment now, Queen Dragon would start to hear the Golden Child's deadly call. Lily patted her scales and spoke some encouraging words in her ear. Suddenly Queen Dragon shuddered in midflight.

"I can't do it, Lily! I can't!"

"You can, Queen Dragon! You can!" Lily

shouted. "You have to do it! For all the dragons who died, you have to do it! Think of them!"

Queen Dragon moaned and flapped her wings uselessly. They started losing height, falling out of the sky toward the river and the killing rocks. For a heart-stopping moment Lily thought they were done for. "Now!" she shrieked. "Do it now, Queen Dragon! Think of me!" And at the last moment Queen Dragon pulled up and, opening her mighty jaws, let blast with a stream of fire in the direction of the cliff.

A thin angry scream sounded over the roar of the flames, but Lily and Queen Dragon ignored it. Orange flame kept pouring from Queen Dragon's mouth until the snow on the cliff top evaporated and the rocks glowed red, cracked, and fell in an avalanche into the water below. The river boiled and clouds of steam enveloped them. If it hadn't been for Mad Brian's fireproof cape, Lily would have been cooked to a cinder. But by the time Queen Dragon's fires were exhausted, the Golden Child was gone, and there was nothing left but a blackened, ravaged section of cliff where it had once stood.

The power of Dragon's Downfall was broken forever.

A week later, back in Ashby, Lily sat at a workbench in the greenhouse at the Liza Cornstalk Memorial Gardens, preparing the blue lily for replanting. Three flowers sat drying on a sheet of blotting paper, and she was carefully cutting into the base of the mother bulb with a scalpel. With luck, next year each cut would grow a baby bulb, giving her four blue lilies instead of one. Soon they would have as many flowers, and as many Quenching Drops, as Ashby needed.

Lily filled a flowerpot with soft brown earth and carefully planted the bulb in it. She sprinkled the pot with water, covered it with a piece of damp burlap, and carefully stood it on a shelf. Somebody tapped on the greenhouse window, and she looked up from her work. Mr. Hartley pulled up the pane and leaned in.

"I'm just letting you know," he said, "that King Lionel has called a special council meeting. It starts in one hour."

"Thanks for telling me," said Lily. "How is Angela getting on?"

"She's very well," said Mr. Hartley. "Pleased to be back, but terribly sad about Gordon. She loved him very much. And even though she hated everything he stood for, in a funny kind of way I think she was fond of the count, too." He paused. "Lionel and Evangeline have apologized to me. So has Tina. Not that I blame any of them for making the mistake. Nobody was to know I'd been looking for Angela for so long when everyone else thought she was dead. We were the only ones who never gave up hope."

"I think that's wonderful," said Lily warmly.

"So do Angela and I," said Mr. Hartley, and he smiled and went off in the direction of the castle.

Lily packed the blue lily pot in her backpack. She went outside, breathed the fresh clean air, and set off with a spring in her step for the Dragon House. Outside it, she found Queen Dragon lying on her back, flicking her tail in time to a scratchy opera record that was starting to wind down.

"That sounds awful!" Lily wound the gramophone handle, and the record sped right up. The singing sounded worse than ever and she put her hands over her ears. Queen Dragon sniffed back a tear.

"Such sad music," she said. "Dragons get such a hard time of it in opera. When I get like this, I like an excuse for a good cry."

"A good cry? Why, Queen Dragon, whatever is the matter?" Lily sat down on the flower-studded grass in front of her.

Queen Dragon shrugged. "Oh, nothing in particular. I was just thinking some sad thoughts about a dragon I used to know."

"Was—was he one of those who died in the war?" Lily asked.

"No. Though he was there at the battle. We were best friends, and when I grew older we planned—well, we were going to be married." Queen Dragon blushed until she glowed. "A dragon wedding is quite something. I'm sorry you'll never get to see one. But then the war came and—you know the rest. Most of the dragons died. But at the height of the battle a few of them managed to escape the Golden Child's call. My friend King Dragon and his companions went through the Eye Stone, just like

Gordon, looking for magical help to end the war. But they never came back."

Lily digested this. "It was an awfully little hole," she said. "How could a dragon possibly get through?"

"Quite easily," said Queen Dragon. "Think back, Lily. You were going to crawl through that hole, weren't you? It would have been a tight fit, but I bet it was just big enough."

"That's right," said Lily.

"And when Gordon went through, he just fit through, too, even though he was taller and quite a bit fatter than you. I think you'd find that if a dragon tried to go through, the same thing would happen."

"You mean," said Lily, starting to understand, "that the hole in the rock gets bigger or smaller depending on who's trying to go through it?"

"That's right." Queen Dragon nodded. "The only problem is, those sorts of magical passages lead to a different destination every time. I don't know where King Dragon ended up, or even when. It might have been a thousand years in the past, or perhaps hundreds of years in the future. Now that I know the Golden Child is gone and that Dragon's Downfall is safe again, maybe one day I'll go and look for him."

"When the time comes I'll help you, Queen Dragon," Lily promised. "You only have to say the word."

"Thank you, Lily," said Queen Dragon. "A dragon couldn't have a truer friend than you."

In the throne room of Ashby Castle, King Lionel's Regal Council had convened. Lionel, Evangeline, Lily, Jason, and Mr. Hartley sat on their carved chairs around the table, and Queen Dragon looked in through the courtyard window. Beside the royal thrones at the end of the table stood another person, someone who in times past had sat on the royal throne himself and ruled in the Black Count's name: the former Captain Zouche.

Lionel stood up. The Great Crown of Ashby sat in its velvet-lined box on the table in front of him. The royal scepter lay beside it, and a large book was open with a pen and inkpot beside it. In front of each member of the council was a golden cup, embossed with the royal arms of Ashby.

"Welcome everybody," said Lionel. "I have called this meeting because Queen Evangeline and I would like to introduce you to our new Royal Councillor, Captain—er, Mr. Zouche. As you all know, Mr. Zouche was the only person apart from Lily Quench who believed in Mr. Hartley during the recent mix-up. You may not know that he also looked after Ashby while Queen Evangeline and I were in the Black Mountains. We thought he should be rewarded for that, so we have also decided to award him the Order of the Boar Spear. Wilibald, if you would kneel?"

Mr. Zouche stepped forward and knelt on a crimson cushion. While everyone else stood watching, Lionel solemnly reached into the box for the Great Crown of Ashby. When he had put it on his head, Queen Evangeline handed him the scepter, and he touched Mr. Zouche lightly on the shoulder.

"Sir Wilibald, I hereby invest you with the Order of the Boar Spear. Do you swear to be loyal to the king and queen of Ashby to your life's end?"

"I swear," growled Zouche.

"Carry the honor bravely," said Lionel, and he leaned forward and pinned a small brown medal on Zouche's jacket. Evangeline kissed him on the cheek and everyone nodded and drank a toast to the new knight.

"Well!" said a voice from the doorway. "This is charming! Back to your old tricks already, I see!"

"Oh, no," muttered Lionel. He cast Evangeline a despairing glance, but it was too late to escape—Crystal was already sweeping into the room. Despite the loss of her mink, she was still looking spectacularly overdressed. In fact, thought Lily, Crystal's sequined gown with its tinkling golden fringe was the most hideous outfit she had ever seen in her life.

"That fringe looks awfully tasty," whispered Queen Dragon through the window.

"I heard that, lizard," said Crystal, "and believe me, you'd better watch your manners. I *am* the Queen Mother, even if my ninny of a son-in-law hasn't had the manners to give me a coronation yet. And after what I've just seen, Evangeline, you've got no excuse. If you can give that fat fool the Order of the Boar Spear—"

Lionel interrupted her. "Actually, Crystal, you've arrived just at the right time. Your title was next on my list."

"It was?" Crystal looked astonished.

"Yes," said Lionel. "As a matter of fact, I think we can give you a new title. Not just yet, but in about six months' time. How does 'Prince's Grandmother' suit you?"

"Prince's Grandmother?" Crystal frowned.

"That's right. Or 'Princess's Grandmother.'"

"But I'm not a grandmother," Crystal protested. "And anyway, I'm far too young—" Suddenly something occurred to her. She stopped and looked at Evangeline suspiciously. "In about six months' time, you say?"

"That's right, Mother," said Evangeline. "Lionel and I are going to have a baby. I don't know why you're looking so surprised."

"I wouldn't have thought he'd have it in him," retorted Crystal.

"*Mother!*" yelled Evangeline. "You might at least look as if you're pleased!"

"I am pleased," said Crystal. "Even if I am too young. But then, I was a child bride."

"If you ask me, it's a wonder she was ever a

bride at all," muttered Queen Dragon. Crystal looked like she was about to explode. Lily hastily jumped up onto her chair and lifted her cup above her head.

"A toast!" she said. "To Crystal, the Royal Grandmother. May her descendants rule Ashby forevermore."

"Amen," said Mr. Hartley.

"To Mother," said Evangeline.

"Hear, hear," said Lionel.

"You'd *better* hear," said Crystal. "Royal Grandmother, hey? Sounds good. I think that merits a pay raise, don't you?"